BOYD COUNTY
AUG 3 0 2023
PUBLIC LIBRARY

WHAT IF...I LOVE YOU

YVONNE MARIE

Sojourner Publishing Group LLC

Copyright © 2023 by Yvonne Marie

All rights reserved.

No part of this publication may be reproduced, distributed, or transmitted in any form or by any means, including photocopying, recording, or other electronic or mechanical methods, without the prior written permission of the publisher, except as permitted by U.S. copyright law.

The story, all names, characters, and incidents portrayed in this production are fictitious. No identification with actual persons (living or deceased), places, buildings, and products is intended or should be inferred.

Book Cover Design by Melody Jeffries

For Ella

Chapter 1

RENEE

THE ONLY THING getting me through this date is imagining all the ways I want to destroy these shoes. I want to give them a death worthy of a high-heel torture device. Why do I do this to myself? I have a whole row of shoes in my closet just like these that I only wear for dates, but they are such a distraction. I'm missing most of what my date is talking about because I can't hear him over the death grip these shoes have on my toes. The noises of the restaurant around us only add to the creeping tension winding up my back.

When I stopped in earlier this week to scope out the restaurant and make a reservation, I specifically requested a table at the back, away from the kitchen and the front door and out of the way of the steady flow of traffic. But when we arrived, a new hostess was on the desk and none of those tables was available, so here we are, near the kitchen, with a steady flow of servers moving past us.

Every time the kitchen door swings open, the sounds of metal pans and clacking utensils fill the air. No one else seems to notice, not even my date sitting across from me, who hasn't stopped talking since we sat down.

I can't decide whether to look at the menu or look at him and at least appear to be interested in what he's saying.

The server is going to come back soon to take our orders and the thought makes me a little anxious. Luckily, I looked over the menu on their website and I plan to either get the seared halibut or the risotto. Both are safe, familiar options.

My date, Kevin, is now telling me about the South America climbing trip he's training for. He relaxes back into his seat, sweeping his hand through his blond hair with an easy grin on his face as he talks. "So I feel I've got the strength-training part down, but endurance is the biggest factor. I've started carrying my pack with me to the gym. I set the treadmill on an incline, and I walk for an hour. It's a great workout."

What do I even say in response to that?

I nod and smile, hoping my smile looks natural. I have the distinct urge to pull out my compact mirror and check, but instead, I keep my hands under the table in my lap, where he can't see the way my fingers attempt to dance away the mounting nervous energy I'm fighting to keep in check.

He hasn't asked a single question. He pauses after every statement like he's waiting for me to applaud or to ask him another question to keep the conversation focused squarely on him. What I'm actually thinking is, *Oh, wow, that's so cool that you're traveling to Peru to climb a mountain alongside thousands of other travelers who are trampling over the natural habitat and ruining the ecosystem, all so you can have this once-in-a-lifetime experience that you will slip into casual conversations for years to come. It will make you so much more interesting.* Of course, that's not what I'm supposed to say. I've been doing this dating thing long enough to know that. I even brainstormed a list of questions and topics to get the conversation flowing. Unfortunately, that list is on my phone, tucked away in my bag, which is hooked onto my chair. Would it be rude to grab it now, in the middle of a conversation? Probably.

The server returns just in time, saving me from having to respond. She swoops over in a cloud of upbeat customer-service energy and Texas charm. "Good evening, my name is Charmaine. I'm your server tonight. I see y'all already got drinks. Are you ready to order?"

I nod and return her smile. This might be the most straightforward part of the date tonight. I grab the menu, open it, and pretend to give it a quick once over.

"I'll have the halibut," I say.

Her eyebrows shoot up. Giving me the first signal that this evening is about to take yet another bad turn.

"Oh, I'm sorry, sweetie. We don't have that on the menu this time of year. You must be thinking about our spring / summer menu."

My stomach sinks. I really look at the menu this time and realize that none of the items on the menu I saw on the website is on this menu.

"Oh, okay," I say flatly. "Uh, Kevin, you order first."

I start scanning the menu for something, anything I like. The problem is that I don't like new things. I'm not an adventurous eater. I have the palate of a twelve-year-old. I eat the same things all the time. If I go out to eat, it's to a restaurant I've been to before and I order the same thing from the menu. But Kevin recommended this place. It's a new, trendy place recently profiled in the *Austin Downtown* magazine. By the time Kevin has placed his order, I've settled on a pasta dish that seems simple enough that I won't hate it.

We place our orders and then Charmaine leaves us. I kind of wish she would stay, maybe pull up a chair. I bet she could come up with something really witty to say about mountain climbing or very easily transition to a new but definitely related topic. Instead, an awkward silence descends over the table as we fumble for something to say to each other.

There has to be a way to make these kinds of first-date dining experiences less uncomfortable. My mind begins to wander to different design possibilities.

"What if each table in a restaurant was its own sensory-regulated dome? You step inside and you're insulated from the noise around you, the conflicting smells, the people brushing by in the aisle." I smile to myself, imagining it. Focusing on solving a problem has always grounded me. I'm so caught up in my imagination that I nearly forget about good old Kevin. But then the kitchen door swings open just as there's a loud crash from inside the kitchen that makes me nearly jump out of my seat.

Kevin stares at me like I'm a circus act. "You're the CEO of Renox Tech, right?" He says it like it's a question, but he clearly already knows the answer.

I thought my transitions were bad.

"Yup," I say before taking a long sip of my water. The ice-cold liquid makes my throat tight as I swallow it down and wait for what I know is coming next.

"That's really cool…"

I look at him—really look at him—maybe for the first time all night. Am I attracted to this person? He looks like every other white guy in the tech scene from Silicon Valley to New York: checkered button-down on a thin, gangly frame and pale skin even though we're living in the Southwest, which tells me he rarely gets outside. Yet he's training to climb a mountain on a treadmill at the gym.

Do I see myself dating him, marrying him, having kids? Having a future with him? Because that's why I'm doing this, right? I'm two years shy of thirty. I have the career that I want, a successful business, a home … but not a partner. Because it always comes down to this…

"I'm a designer, too, actually."

I just nod a "mm-hm" and wait for it.

"I have this great idea I'd like to run by you."

And there it is.

Even though I saw it coming, it doesn't hurt any less. He's not here because he wants to date me. He's here because he Googled me and saw that I'm the youngest CEO of an education tech firm in the country and he wants to pitch me his Big Idea.

I prepare myself to sit stiffly through the pitch, to nod and smile, offer encouragement, even agree to take a look at his deck and give feedback, and suffer all the way through the end of the meal. And the thought makes me feel queasy.

I pretend a lot.

I pretend to be comfortable and confident and relaxed. And on nights like this, I feel the weight of all that pretending. I feel the cost of giving more than I ever get back from guys like Kevin.

Charmaine comes back with our meals and a broad smile on her face like she's delivering us the answer to our dreams.

Before she can set it on the table, I say, "Can I get mine to go? And the check, please." The smile instantly drops from Charmaine's face and she looks at Kevin like it must be his fault. I almost make an excuse and come to his defense, but I stop myself.

Kevin rears back like he's been slapped. "Is everything okay? Don't leave. We just got our meals and I'd love to chat with you more about—"

Nope. I slap some bills on the table. "Never mind. I honestly didn't even want pasta tonight."

I grab my leather tote and pull out the flip-flops that I put in my bag before leaving the house. Quickly, I yank the torture shoes off my feet and slide into my flip-flops. My feet sing with relief. All the while, Kevin is babbling, trying to salvage this date, but I'm moments away from freedom and I don't hear a word he's saying.

Chapter 2

RENEE

"I'M DONE WITH DATING," I tell my best friend, Jordyn.

Last night, I went home and tossed out every pair of uncomfortable shoes I owned. I'm done wearing shoes that pinch my feet, and I'm done going on dates with men who only end up wanting something from me: a job, access to my network, a woman to take care of them and help them accomplish their dreams.

They always want something but it's never me. From now on, I'm focusing on the things that give my life meaning. Namely, my company, Renox Tech. I don't know why I ever thought I need a relationship to make me happy. There's only ever been one man who made me feel like I was something special, someone worth choosing, and even he left.

Jordyn raises a perfectly arched eyebrow and waits for me to elaborate. Today my friend has fire-engine red hair falling in layers around her beautiful brown face. Last month, I think it was jet black with green layers. She pushes her tortoiseshell cat eyeglasses up her lightly freckled noise and asks, "What do you mean, you're giving up dating? Was the date that bad?"

Jordyn has been one of my best friends since we met in undergrad at the University of Texas. She has seen me through every phase of my dating life. Like in sophomore year, when I would lurk around and watch my crushes, too shy and awkward to speak to them. Or that phase right after college when I would date the fun but unreliable guys like my ex, Jonathan, who was an experiment in proving I could be the chill, no-expectations kind of girlfriend.

Now that I've built a somewhat notable career as a product designer working in the education and disability space, I find myself meeting more and more guys who turn out to just be opportunists looking for a chance to use me to get ahead.

"Kevin was a designer with an idea to pitch."

"What! Again? Ugh. What is up with these dudes? I'm so sorry, Renee. But come on, you can't give up. You deserve happiness."

I shake my head over my coffee mug. "I am happy. And that's why I'm done with dating. I have everything that I need right here. I'm going to focus on what works well in my life: my work."

Jordyn gives me a long look like she's preparing to argue, but whatever she sees in my eyes makes her think better of it.

Thankfully she drops it and we move on to listing priorities for the day. After we finish strategizing, Jordyn hops up from the chair and heads back to her desk. Today she's wearing a retro fifties-style floral swing dress that somehow manages to not look completely out of place in the offices of a boutique tech-design firm.

One of the things I admire most about Jordyn is her ability to be fully herself, no matter what room she's in. I wish I had that kind of relaxed confidence. Fortunately, Jordyn has enough for both of us. I couldn't run this company without her.

Which is why it sucks to know this will be her last week working with me.

Before she exits the office, I call, "Hey!"

She turns with a smile on her face to look at me expectantly.

"Are you sure you don't want to stay?" I plead.

Jordyn went right into teaching after graduation, but after three years of working in struggling, underfunded schools, she left feeling burned out and disillusioned about the public education system. I offered her a job at Renox Tech as an operations manager and design advisor while she got back on her feet. She's consulted on several projects and her classroom experience has made her input invaluable. Turns out that working here was exactly what she needed to renew her passion for education, and now she's heading into the school system as a learning specialist. I'm happy for her but anxious about not having the one person who truly understands me by my side every day.

She sighs and nods. "You've got this, Renee. You ran this place without me and you can do it again."

Problem is, I'm not sure I want to. I nod and give her a half-hearted smile before turning back to focus on my work.

I put on my noise-canceling headphones and choose an ambient-beats playlist. Time flies when I'm in hyper-focused mode, so I'm not surprised when I look and see that two hours have passed.

I peek through the glass that separates my office from the rest of the office. The Renox Tech offices are mostly open-space industrial-style offices with large farm-style wooden tables that serve as workspaces. The tall loft windows invite natural light to flow in around the room. I watch my small staff of five moving between spaces, hovering around computers to chat and collaborate.

Jordyn is my operations manager in title, but really, she manages the entire staff because I'm not good at it, nor do I like having to manage other people.

When Jordyn came on board a year ago, it was such a relief to turn staff supervision over to her so I could focus on the work. But as I sit in my own office watching the staff interact with each other, I feel a bit like an outsider in my own company.

The minute I walk out of my office and enter their domain, the energy will shift. The laughter and conversation will end, everyone will go back to their own desks, and the nods and smiles they toss me will be slightly more reserved than when they talk with each other. I know part of it is because I'm the boss, the one who signs their paychecks, but I think it's so much more. I wish socializing came more naturally to me, but it never has.

It wasn't until I was diagnosed with autism in my first year of college that I began to understand why I always felt like an outsider in every space, why all my attempts at behaving the way other kids my age did seemed to only make my differences that much more pronounced.

When I try to participate in the fun, it comes out awkward and forced. So instead, I hide in my office and watch from a distance.

Around noon, my stomach starts to rumble and I know I can't hide much longer. I leave my office and head to the kitchen, keeping my eyes forward and hoping to get in and out undetected.

An open-floor-plan office was never my preference, but our work is so collaborative that it makes sense, especially since the space is too small for more than one separate office.

"Hey, Renee."

What If...I Love You

My stomach clenches. I turn to look at Davis, a senior designer.

Whatever he sees on my face makes him hesitate. "Uh, I'm sorry. Is this a good time to talk?"

"Oh, yes, yes, of course. What's up, Davis?" I try to infuse some lightness into my tone and rearrange my face into what I hope is a pleasant expression.

"I was wondering if I could talk through some ideas I have for this new supportive learning portal we're designing for the university."

"Of course."

I follow him over to his desk, all the while wondering what my face is doing. Do I look relaxed?

Davis sits in front of his computer while I inch closer to stand over him. He looks up, slightly confused. "Uh, you want to sit down?"

I freeze for a moment, unsure of what to do, and then Jordyn slides a chair right under my legs and I sit abruptly. "Okay, let's see what you got."

The conversation with Davis goes well. Or, at least, I think it does. We spend about thirty minutes tossing ideas back and forth and I help him work through some of the issues he was struggling with about making the portal more accessible for student users. I encourage him to do another test run of the portal with a focus group of users. Because that's how we work at Renox. We use a participatory design approach that involves users early in the design process to ensure we create products that will respond to their needs.

I head back into my office after my conversation with Davis feeling great. Maybe I'll start doing regular brainstorming sessions with the team or make time to collaborate and support their different projects.

As I eat my lunch at my desk, I decide to open social media

and scroll a bit while I munch on my salad. What I see makes me nearly drop my food in my lap.

I am a trending hashtag on ChitChat, and that is never a good thing.

"Jordyn!"

Hearing the panic in my voice, Jordyn rushes in. "What's wrong?"

"I ... I ... What's happening?" I just point at the screen, unable to make sense of what I'm seeing. "Why are they saying these things about me?"

Jordyn looks at the screen and all the color drains from her face. It's all I need to see to know that I've just been canceled.

Chapter 3

KNOX

"SO, as you can see, last quarter we saw a fifteen-percent increase in profits. Which is the slowest rate of growth that we've seen in nearly a decade. But it's nothing to worry about. We knew this would happen after your, uh … father passed away. Our shareholders just need to get to know you and then they will see that they can trust you just as they trusted your father."

I look up from the sales report in front of me toward Jeffrey Marsh, LyonTech's CFO. "Are you saying it's my fault our profits are slowing?"

Jeffrey sighs and adjusts his thick black-rimmed glasses on his long, straight nose. "I'm saying that nobody likes change. It's just taking everyone time to adjust." He raises an eyebrow and shoots a glance toward our board president, Michael. Clearly, they aren't confident I'm settling into my new role as CEO of LyonTech, the firm founded by my father thirty years ago. These two men may not have been at the founding, but they've been by my father's side for more than twenty years and they watched me grow up along the way. I'm pretty sure they're more than a little pissed that I was named his successor, and not one of them.

Six months ago, just before my father died after a long battle with cancer, the board was forced to announce that I was taking over his role as CEO.

It wasn't a surprise to me; my father had been preparing me for the role for nearly four years. But it was a surprise to his CFO and board president.

My father not only hid the fact that he was sick but put a succession plan in place that neither of them was privy to. Turns out he didn't trust them as much as they thought. I'm still not sure why my father was so determined to make sure I took over his company when there were far more qualified people who were loyal to him and to his vision. But when he made it clear to me that these were his final wishes, I dropped everything to come work for him and to prepare to step into this role.

It was a steep learning curve, especially for someone fresh out of college, but I couldn't let him down. I won't let him down, no matter what anyone says. I'm going to figure out how to be the CEO my father believed I could be and make sure to protect his legacy. But in order to do that, I need to put our board and shareholders at ease, or this ship will sink when I've only barely taken over the helm.

"Okay, I get it. Change is hard." I nod and smile, attempting to convey more confidence than I feel. "I'm a new face and everyone is holding their breath to see what I'll do. Well, I don't intend to fail. This is my father's legacy and there is no one more determined to protect what he built than me. Is there anything else, Jeffrey?"

"Uh, yes, there is one more thing." Jeffrey begins shuffling papers, looking a little hesitant to continue. "If we want your tenure as CEO to get off to a strong start and not lose any shareholders, it's important that you send a strong message communicating your vision for LyonTech. You're a young, energetic new face of the company and you need to position yourself alongside the Zuckerbergs and Dorseys of the tech world, as a leader building highly scalable and profitable tech solutions. We'd like to craft a message for you. Present some ideas on potential new product launches that would get our shareholders excited about what LyonTech brings to the marketplace."

I was totally on board with what he was saying for a moment, aside from the part where he compared me to social media company founders. That's not even remotely in the realm of what we do at LyonTech. We have twenty thousand patents in the vault for useable tech that people take for granted, like touchscreen glass and night-vision scopes used by the military. We're piloting new technology in the AR space that is revolutionizing mental health care. We're the old guard of technology built on hardware, not social experiences. But he's not wrong. I should be thinking about what my vision is for the company.

I need to build on the very solid foundation that my father has built to create something new. Something that could improve the lives of so many people. That's the reason why I went into this business in the first place. I wanted to use tech to reduce inequality and create social change. But as I listen to Jeffrey, what makes me tighten my jaw is that he's just suggested that they would craft this vision for me, like I'm some kind of empty-brained figurehead. I'm not here to be a fucking showpiece. I've been preparing for this role for four years. I may not have the experience they have from working alongside my father for decades, but the fact is he chose me, not them. I may not understand his reasoning fully, but I know he wouldn't have set me up to fail.

I let out a slow breath and relax my jaw.

"No."

Jeffrey's eyebrows shoot up to his nonexistent hairline. "What do you mean, no?"

"I will craft the message. But first, I need time to review existing product pipelines and decide what I want my main stage offering to be."

Michael shifts in his seat and straightens his tie, suddenly deciding to join the conversation. For a minute, I was really wondering why he is even here. He's been checking his phone for the last forty minutes like he has more important things to do. He's a small man—at five foot seven, he barely reaches my shoulders—but he makes up for his lack of stature with a sharp ability to read people and quickly target their weaknesses.

He turns his piercing blue eyes and condescending smirk on me and clears his throat. "Listen, kiddo. I know you want to take this job seriously, but in order to do that, you have to let us help you. We both advised your father for years. The reason he was so successful was that he trusted us to help him. Now, you need to trust that we know how to steer this ship and keep LyonTech on course."

My whole body seethes with fire. Did this asshole just call me kiddo? I'm moments away from losing my cool, but that's exactly what he wants. He wants me to act like a spoiled brat and have a tantrum just to prove his point.

I stand up from my seat and walk to the wall of floor-to-ceiling windows behind my desk. I can feel my dad's presence in this room. I've yet to remove his things from the office. There are signs of him everywhere: the rich mahogany wood desk that I now call my own, the high-back leather chair still molded to his body from ages of use. Even his scent of lavender and bergamot still faintly lingers in the room.

I need you, son. His words the day I learned he was sick still echo in the back of my mind. Every time I feel my confidence waning, every time I worry that maybe I've made a mistake in taking on this role, I hear his voice cracking open with a vulnerability that I'd never heard from him before. In this moment, it makes me want to protect everything that he was.

With my back to them, I speak slowly, the way I've seen my father do so many times when he was leaving zero room for misinterpretation.

"Michael, I get it. You have been around a long time. Jeffrey, you too. You understand this company inside and out. I believe that you think you know the best way for us to move forward. But…" I finally turn to face them, having fully composed myself again. Out of the corner of my eye, I see my assistant, Martin, rushing down the hall toward my office. I pause mid-thought. If Martin is running in here in the middle of a meeting, it must be an emergency. At first I think it's my mother, and a cold wave of dread descends over me. I can't lose her too. Not now.

"I'm sorry to interrupt, but you're going want to see this," he says breathlessly. He crosses to the TV, snatches up the remote, and turns it on. The wave of dread quickly recedes but now my face is frozen in confusion. What the hell is going on?

The voice of a news correspondent fills the room, and as I watch, it only takes a moment to realize that he's standing outside our offices. Behind him is a small group of protesters with signs.

"It began with one post on a popular social-media messaging app that turned into a public outcry against unethical tech targeting the disabled. The multinational firm LyonTech is the manufacturer of the Calm Monitor, a biometric monitor designed by education tech designer and FutureForward 30 Under 30 Innovator of the Year Renee Johnson. Johnson sold the technology to LyonTech, which is now preparing to distribute it to residential treatment facilities Caldwell Homes. Caldwell is currently under investigation for the abuse of patients in their facilities. Disability advocates say LyonTech has a responsibility to end their deal with Caldwell and immediately stop production on the device."

By the time the news reporter has wrapped up and moved on to a new topic, I am reeling.

Michael looks pissed. "I guarantee you one of our competitors is behind this. They see that we're weak, that we're in a moment of transition, and they're trying to take advantage of it."

I'm stunned. First of all, how did I not know that we had bought one of Renee's designs? Just hearing her name is like a paddle shock to the chest.

"Martin, get me everything on the Calm Monitor and the Caldwell deal. I need to get up to speed on this."

Michael swings his head toward me so quickly, he might have given himself whiplash. "If you're thinking about canceling the deal with Caldwell, I suggest you think again."

Jeffrey steps between us, hands raised like a referee in an MMA match. "Listen, we've just received a lot of information. Emotions are running high. We don't need to make any decisions right now—we just need to get the full picture of what is going on and come up with a response. Let's get legal and PR on the phone and come up with a measured response. The last thing we want is to appear rolled over by some woke Gen Z activists who have no idea what they're talking about. I'm sure this will all blow over in a day or two."

What they're saying barely registers. All I can think about is Renee. Her name was mentioned. She was the creator of the device. There's no way she's not feeling the heat too. But she doesn't have a legal and PR department to help her navigate this situation. "I think whatever our response, we need to coordinate with Renee and the Renox Tech team. They're just as much a part of this."

"Renee Johnson. Isn't that your old business partner?" Jeffrey asks tentatively.

I nod. "Yes, we co-founded Renox Tech together."

"Okay, you're right. Let's give them a set of talking points. I'm sure we had her sign an NDA so she'll just need to follow our lead," Michael says while texting on his phone.

I turn to glare at him. Hearing him talk about Renee so dismissively makes me want to reach across my desk, snatch him up by his collar, and shove that phone down his throat. Instead, I take another breath and unclench my jaw.

"I'll talk to Renee myself. Figure out how to reduce the blowback on her. Renox Tech is a small firm. Something like this could sink them." The problem is, I have no idea how I'll get her to talk to me.

After they reluctantly leave my office, I settle back into the chair that used to be my father's and turn to face the floor-to-ceiling glass windows. *You chose me, Dad. I just wish I knew why, and what I'm supposed to do to make this job my own while preserving your legacy.* This situation with Renee and Caldwell only makes everything more complicated.

Martin returns with a stack of reports on the Calm Monitor and the Caldwell deal. He tells me the team running this contract is ready to meet whenever I call them.

For the next hour, I dig into the documents, trying to understand what the Calm Monitor is and why it's being sold to Caldwell. But my thoughts keep turning back to Renee. We were best friends who became business partners fresh out of college.

Even though I didn't stick around to help her build it, I can't help but feel protective of the company we founded together. Not just for the company, but for our friendship. We worked so well together. We complemented each other in every way.

I've missed her so much.

But when my father got sick, I left, and I couldn't even tell her why because my father demanded that I keep his secret. Even made me sign an NDA.

My own father.

Knowing that Renee is dealing with this all on her own makes me itch to reach out to her now. To go to her door and refuse to leave until she lets me in; let me finally explain why I had to walk away from her and what we built. But even as I had the thought, I knew I would be standing on her doorstep for a long time before she ever even looked at me. Because that's how stubborn Renee is. I even miss that most annoying trait of hers. I wish she had come to me when she was thinking about selling to LyonTech. I would have done everything in my power to make sure the deal went down the way she wanted.

There's simply no way Renee would have agreed to have her product sold to a place like Caldwell. Now I have to figure out a way to keep this storm from destroying my reputation as the new CEO of LyonTech, and taking Renox Tech down in the process.

I pick up the phone to call the one person I know who can help me to reconnect with Renee.

Chapter 4

RENEE

I'M A PROBLEM SOLVER.

It's why I became a product designer. All around me, every day, I see things that could be improved. Systems that could be more efficient. Everyday appliances that, with a small change to the user experience, would take care of the minor pain points that cause frustration.

I live in the possibility of things being better, more useful, more efficient. But as I sit here on my couch on day three of my self-imposed exile, reviewing every single note, report, and plan for the Calm Monitor, I can't see it. I just can't see how I could have gotten this so wrong. What makes it hurt so much more is the fact this was a very personal project for me.

The Calm Monitor was meant to improve the lives of nonspeaking disabled people and their families. We did focus groups with dozens of parents and caregivers who were excited about the possibility of having a biometric monitor that would alert them to the physiological distress signals of their loved ones, all from an app on their phone. It's meant to be a noninvasive way to make sure that a nonspeaking person's needs aren't neglected when they most need support. Interventions in moments of distress could begin more quickly, reducing the long-term impact of chronic stress.

My mistake was selling it to LyonTech. There's no way I could have known that they would sell the technology to a place like Caldwell. Caldwell Homes is one the largest managers in the country of residential treatment facilities for people with neurological disorders. They're currently facing a class-action lawsuit led by families who claim Caldwell used traumatic restrictive and punitive techniques to control and abuse patients.

I only sold the patent to LyonTech because I thought they were better positioned to get the Calm Monitor out to families, caregivers, and schools. I never intended for it to be used by a place like Caldwell. Now, here I am, suffering the backlash of their decision. A decision, no doubt, driven by profits.

I wonder if he was involved in this decision.

Knox.

My former best friend and business partner. The co-founder of Renox Tech who walked away four years ago, leaving me to run the company alone.

It's hard to believe he would put profits before people. But then again, I never thought he leave me to go work with LyonTech.

It's only when I stretch my legs beneath me that I feel how stiff my body is.

When did I last move? Or eat? I take a sniff of my hoodie. Or bathe?

Three days. Three days of sitting here, trying to find the problem. Trying to find a solution that won't destroy everything I worked for. I won't let him take this from me too.

Even in the shower, my mind doesn't rest. I cycle through

What If...I Love You

every phase of the design process, trying to figure out if there was something I missed as I scrub three days of grit off my skin. My brain snags onto something. A statement that one caregiver made in one of my final focus groups. Focus groups I insisted on leading myself because of how personal this project is to me. Plus, who better to empathize with the parents of autistic kids than me? An autistic kid who can look back now and see all the ways that my mom struggled to take care of me. Struggled to understand my needs. I remember her breaking down into tears of frustration, trying to understand why I was having a meltdown when I was unable to explain to her what was wrong. Until I was seven, I didn't speak. I learned sign language, but rarely would I use it to communicate. She tried to communicate with me and probably never expected me to speak. But then, at seven, I started talking in fully formed sentences, as if I had always been speaking. I still hadn't been diagnosed or diagnosed properly, but I had plenty of misdiagnoses up until that point.

So it had to be me who led the focus-group conversations. What I heard, for the most part, aligned with everything I thought about how the monitor should work, what its purpose was, and how it would improve the lives of nonspeakers and their caregivers. For the most part. But now I recall there was one outlier. I don't even think I even wrote it down, but I can see the moment so clearly in my mind now. One person, a caregiver—the sister of a nonspeaking autistic person—asked about something, something that was outside of what the monitor was capable of. "Why doesn't the monitor allow people to address their own needs?" At the time, I dismissed it. I kept thinking about my mom. I designed it with caregivers like her in mind.

I step out of the bathroom post-shower, but instead of feeling refreshed, the heavy weight of exhaustion settles over me. I'm coming down from the stress and the hyper-focus on searching for a solution.

I grab a fresh pair of sweatpants and a sweater and get dressed.

Next, I try to eat, but nothing in my refrigerator looks remotely appetizing. I've subsisted on shrimp fried rice the last two days, and I know I can't keep that up much longer. But I don't have much of an appetite. I'm still staring into the refrigerator, trying to decide what to eat, when my phone rings.

My entire body instantly tightens. The only people who have called me besides Jordyn the past three days have been reporters wanting a comment or an interview or a reaction to something a stranger has said about me on the internet. I still don't know what to say. I take a peek at the caller ID and see that it's just my mom. But even that doesn't give me any relief.

For a moment, I debate whether to let it go to voicemail, but I know that I won't call her back. I grab my phone, head into the kitchen, and answer the phone.

"Hello, my sweet girl."

I place the phone on speaker and set it on the kitchen counter. Despite my exhaustion, it is nice to hear my mom's voice. She has a sweet, soothing voice that sounds like she should be leading a guided meditation, but it's just that Northern California vibe that I somehow never managed to master.

"Hey, Mama." In the background, I can hear that familiar soft rustling sound. She's probably in her backyard with her hands deep in soil. "What are you doing?"

"Just working in the garden. Oh, honey, you should see the asters this year. They are gorgeous and the blue fescues are so vivid, you feel like you're on an acid trip!" Mom is a gardener and herbalist. She has an apothecary where she sells locally harvested medicinal herbs, tonics, and tinctures. After telling me about the wild lavender she foraged on one of her recent hikes, she turns the conversation back to me. "I heard about what happened. Everyone makes mistakes, honey. Even you."

What is that supposed to mean? My only mistake was selling to LyonTech.

"I'm sure this will all blow over soon enough. People have such short attention spans. They will move on to being outraged by something new next week. You are too bright a star to let something like this dim your light. Not many young people can start a successful business right out of college and … you did that."

I notice she's quick to omit Knox. Mom loved Knox. Whenever we went to visit, he'd spend time with her in the garden, tagging along on her wildcrafting missions in the woods and bringing home huge jars of dried herbs for tea. He was like the son she never had. I never showed the kind of interest in her work that he did. In fact, having him there was a relief sometimes because it took the pressure off me.

"I hope you're taking some time off while this whole hullabaloo blows over. Be kind to yourself, baby."

"I know, Mama. I am. I'm actually going to be leading another hike and camping trip soon."

"That's nice." After a pause, she says, "This might be a good time to go back to therapy."

My stomach clenches at the mention of therapy. When I was in high school, she sent me to therapy. It led to a string of misdiagnoses that only increased my confusion and anxiety. First I was depressed, then bipolar, and it wasn't until a doctor suggested I might have a personality disorder that my mother finally stopped making me go. Then it was just positive affirmations, self-esteem workshops for girls, and summer programs for the special and gifted. Finally getting my autism diagnosis in college was like being offered a road map to understanding myself for the first time in my life. But for my mom, it has been much harder to accept. To her, autistics are socially awkward white men, not shy, academically gifted Black girls from the Bay.

She sighs and softens her voice a little. "I just think that a change in perspective—"

"It's not about reframing my thinking," I cut her off. "I can't think my way out of being autistic, Mom."

"Oh, honey, that's not what I'm suggesting ... but I did read a book recently that I want to send to you. It's about Highly Sensitive People. I think it's a much better description of you."

A buzzing swarms up my chest, quickly wrapping around my throat, threatening to choke me. I can't even hear my mother talk. *No, no, no, no.* I want to scream at her, but I can't. My anger is immediately doused by the more familiar feeling of guilt and shame. She means well. She's the only parent I have. She took care of me alone and I wasn't an easy child to raise. The silence, the meltdowns, the obsessive focus on only the things I cared about. She didn't understand my needs, but she did her best.

"Mom, thanks for calling but I have to go. I'll call you later."

"Are you okay, baby?"

"I'm fine. I just ... I just have to go. Love you." I quickly hang up the phone.

It's like the floor quickly rises up to meet me, or maybe my legs fail to hold me up. But every muscle in my body feels taut and I need to sit. I close my eyes, count, and rock. I promise myself that when I get to one hundred, I will get up off the floor, make a meal—the first I'll eat all day—and begin to make a plan. I close my eyes and press my hands to my eyes and press down until I see sparks of light behind my eyelids. And I count.

Chapter 5

RENEE

A WEEK GOES by and I barely leave the couch. I can't seem to get up. I can't decide if it's because I'm depressed or maybe I'm more burnt out than I realized.

I've been rewatching episodes of *The Opening* and *Clone Wars*, taking comfort in storylines that I've just about memorized after watching each show from beginning to end at least five times. I'm deep into episode six of season four of *The Opening*, watching Hyacinth Walker make the decision that will lead to the rise of the space terrorist Rex Donovan, when my phone vibrates on the coffee table. It's another number I don't recognize so I cancel the call and turn back to my show.

Outside I can hear the rain that began yesterday picking up. Even though it's early, barely eight a.m., the sky looks unnaturally dark. I look at the balcony glass doors and watch the rain fall. The wind has knocked my balcony furniture over, but I can't bring myself to care or do anything about it.

I couldn't sleep last night. My mind was an endless cycle of invasive thoughts. Before I left the office the day everything fell apart, Jordyn took my phone, removed all my social media apps, and made me promise that I would not go on to read the endless barrage of comments about me, LyonTech, and the Calm Monitor.

I've never hidden the fact that I am autistic, but it's also not something I usually talk about publicly. If I was more public about my neurodivergence, would that change what they think of me? Would they understand why I designed the Calm Monitor?

So far, I've avoided going online. Not until I know what to say. Not until I find a solution. But it's been a week, hiding out at home, and I've got nothing.

I head into the kitchen to make some coffee. Filling the kettle with water to boil, I grab the coffee beans and add three scoops of the whole beans into the coffee grinder. Before turning on the coffee grinder, I slide in the earplugs that I keep in the kitchen. The loud grating sound fills the quiet kitchen, nearly drowning out the sound of the rain for ten seconds as the beans are reduced to coarse grounds. Just as the kettle starts its low hum, I remove it from the stovetop and combine the coffee grounds and water in my French press, stirring the coffee and checking the clock to begin timing the brewing process. In exactly seven minutes, my coffee will be ready.

I love a perfectly timed routine.

What if ... a French press came with a built-in time? I grab my phone and quickly search it. Yup, already exists. I leave the tab open so I can remember to buy one later.

I grab my favorite mug from the shelf above the sink. The mug I've drunk my coffee, and only my coffee, in ever since Knox bought it for me during one of our road trips years ago. We drove to Mount Bonnell—about a two-hour drive outside the city. It was the weekend after we graduated from college.

What If...I Love You

We were already living together. After all the graduation festivities had finally died down and we started to settle into post-college life, we packed up Knox's SVU and drove out to the mountain.

We hiked for hours, barely speaking, just moving in sync up the mountain. Knox was always one of the few people I could be with and not feel like I needed to fill the silence with small talk. We didn't need to talk to feel like we were doing something together. We could just walk along a trail together with the sound of the ground crunching beneath our feet and our inhale and exhale with each step.

On the way back, we stopped at a gas station. I sat in the passenger seat as Knox went in to grab snacks for the ride. When he came out, he handed me a mug. "Graduate" was written in white letters against a black mug. I've used it ever since. I have little reminders of him like that all around me, no matter how hard I'd like to forget. To move on from us.

I look around the open living / dinner area, struck by how much of myself I see in this space despite the fact that I've spent nearly every waking moment working on my business. Along one expanse of wall is the large bookcase filled with the books that have been my constant companion since I was a child. There's the comfy brown leather chair by the fireplace that I splurged on at Jordyn's insistence, and the long wooden dinner table I found through a small woodworking shop in Tennessee that sits parallel to the kitchen island. The table seats six, and though I've never had that many people in my house, I love the length of the table, the thickness of the wood, the texture and line of the wood telling you the history of the tree it was carved from. As I walk around the space, I realize that I spent so much time decorating and organizing the space, yet I've never truly taken the time to enjoy it.

I'm sitting at the dining room table with my coffee, facing the balcony, watching the rain fall, when I hear it. The wind whistles outside and a chair crashes into the glass door, finally making my decision to bring the balcony furniture inside before it flies away. When I open the balcony doors, I'm immediately assaulted by the rain as it whips across my face like tiny needle pricks. I stand there for a moment, appreciating the pressurized feeling of wet and cold across my skin. It's the first thing I've felt, besides a pendulum swing between numbness and anxiety, all week. I quickly grab the two chairs and the table and drag them back inside.

It's only when I close the balcony door that I hear it. The slow, steady trickle that isn't coming from outside. It's inside. There's water dripping inside my townhouse.

I get up to investigate, following the sound of the drip to the laundry room down the hall. I look up; the plaster is sagging under the weight of the water. A slow trickle is coming from the peak. It's only a matter of time before it gets worse. Panic rises in my chest, but I tamp it down long enough to unplug the washer and dryer. Then I grab a bucket from the small closet where I keep all the cleaning supplies and place it under the leak.

The panic continues to rise like a cold wave over my skin as I pace the hall outside the laundry room, watching the leak grow more and more aggressive. Instinctively, I begin to deepen my breathing, placing my hand over my belly, summoning the tools I've learned to calm myself in moments of overwhelm.

I can do this. I can do this.

But my thoughts are such a swirling jumble that I can't figure out what to do. Just figure out step one, I tell myself. Step one. Step one. What is it? Call a roofer. I move back to the dining area where my laptop is and open it up. When I first moved in, I put together a list of contractors to do some minor work on my house. One of them handled roofs. I find his number and am ready to dial when I notice the time. It's only

7:15 a.m.. There is no way they're open yet. I go to the website for McCallen Contractors and, sure enough, they don't open until nine a.m.

What the hell am I supposed to do in the meantime?

An hour passes with me pacing back and forth from the laundry room, watching the leak grow worse. The bucket quickly fills with water. I dump it and start again. All the while, anxiety weighs heavy in my stomach as I go through every possible scenario of what I can do. I research several other contractors who handle roof repairs. Read reviews. Watch YouTube videos on roof leaks and the process of patching them. I think about what it might cost me to do the repair and how that will eat into what little savings I've been able to put aside. The rain continues its assault outside. It's not expected to stop for another three hours. How much worse will the leak get before that happens?

Around eight thirty, there is loud crack, followed by a gush of water. I race back to the laundry room as the water begins to spill out into the hallway.

No!

I freeze, watching as the water covers my hardwood floors and spreads in every direction.

No. No. No. No. No.

Time passes. But I'm frozen in my spot, my mind a whirlwind of thoughts moving so quickly I feel like I'm trapped in a tornado as the hurricane outside rages on. I'm not sure how long I stand there, just watching the water spread.

The sound of my phone ringing snaps me out of it and I breathe again. It must be Jordyn, calling to check in.

"Jordyn, it's … it's everywhere. I can't stop it. I don't know what to do."

"Renee, slow down. Are you okay?"

I look at the phone, confused, because that is not Jordyn's

voice. Even without the name popping up on my screen, I know that voice.

"Knox?"

"Yeah, it's me."

I hang up immediately and stare at the phone.

It rings again. I answer with a frustrated grunt.

"Renee, please don't hang up!"

"What do you want, Knox? This isn't a good time." I'm practically panting as I speak, my anxiety ratcheting up as the water continues to spread. Hearing the voice of the one person I never expected to ever speak to again isn't helping.

"Tell me what's going on. You don't sound good."

"I … I … there's water everywhere. The roof, it … it's not your problem. I need to get out of here."

"Where are you going?"

"I don't know!"

"I know you don't like to drive in the rain. I'll help you sort out the leak and then you can come to my place until it's fixed."

"Absolutely not. You're the last person I want to see. I'll call Jordyn."

"Jordyn's out of town."

"I'll get a hotel room until I can sort this out."

"No. Don't move. I'm on my way. I'll be there in fifteen minutes."

"What? How do you even know where I live?" He doesn't respond and I don't need him to. I already know Jordyn told him.

"Renee, don't move. You can be pissed at me. You don't even have to speak to me, but I'm coming to get you. Pack a bag and be ready in fifteen minutes." He hangs up the phone.

I stare at my phone, trying to figure out what just happened. The ex-friend ex-business partner I haven't spoken to in four years is now the person coming to my rescue in the middle of a full-on meltdown as my beautiful townhouse is destroyed by a flood. The water doesn't stop flowing. I can't begin to think about all the damage. One thing at a time. Get out of this house, and then deal with Knox reappearing in my life.

I quickly begin moving things off the floor and bottom shelves of my bookcases, trying to save as many things as I can. Some of my furniture will be damaged; some might be salvaged if the water doesn't get too bad. I tread through the water that now comes to my ankles and seeps toward my bedroom. Luckily, it's up a short flight of stairs on the other side of the house.

I grab my phone and pull up the rideshare app. There are no cars in the area. It could be at least sixty minutes before one arrives. Hopefully, Knox will be slowed down by the storm. Maybe roads are flooded and he won't even be able to get into my neighborhood. Never have I ever prayed for flooded roads, downed trees, anything to waylay my former best friend from getting here.

Unfortunately, there is a knock on my door exactly fifteen minutes later. I hesitate for a moment, hoping he might just turn around and leave.

"I know you're in there. Open the door, Renee! I'm not leaving until you do."

I sigh, staring at the front door, imagining him standing on the other side, probably drenched. I finally move toward the door.

"Knox, go away. I don't need your help. I can deal with this on my own."

"I know you can, but you don't have to. Also, I'm biologically incapable of not showing up when you need me."

I bark a laugh into the closed door. "You walked away when I needed you most. Showing up today doesn't change that."

There's a pause and for a moment I think he's going to walk away. Again.

"You're right. But one thing at a time. You have a leak. The rain isn't going to stop for a while. A contractor won't come out until it does. In the meantime, it's not safe for you to stay here. Please let me help you."

I know he's right and being stubborn; resisting his help will only make things worse.

One thing at a time.

I open the door. His broad frame fills the doorway. He quickly steps in past me and begins looking around.

"Okay, it's not too bad. There will be some damage. You'll have to get the floors replaced but you won't lose much. I brought some cinder blocks and milk crates to put your furniture on to keep anything you want to save out of the water."

"Where did you get cinder blocks?"

"Ha! Don't ask." He smiles his Knox smile, all charm and light, absent the playful dancing and the hint of mischief in his hazel eyes. Right now, he looks serious. Concerned. *Different*. His hair is shorter. His beard looks well groomed, like he goes to one of those fancy bespoke barber shops to be wrapped in a steaming towel before a straight razor sculpts the hair on his face into perfect symmetry. His rain jacket is wet and sticks to his broad shoulders and athletic build from years of playing sports.

For a moment, I just stand there and stare up at him and he looks back. Even though he's at least half a foot taller than me, I never used to feel small when I was with him. But right now, the intensity in his eyes makes me want to shrink and hide. I quickly turn away from his intense gaze and continue grabbing things off the floor.

"Knox, please leave. I can do this on my own. I think you and your company have done more than enough. I'm so angry, I can't even look at you right now."

But that's a lie. I want to look at him. I miss looking at him, and anger isn't what I'm feeling in this moment. It's something else. Something that makes me feel like there is a fifty-pound weight sitting on my chest and an invisible vise around my throat.

Knox takes a step toward me and I instinctively step back. The distance is all I have left and I'm holding on to it like a tether that will keep my anger righteous and targeted.

"Renee, there is so much you don't know. So much I need to explain to you. But first, we need to get you out of here and someplace safe and dry. Let me help you and then we can talk it all out."

I'm shaking my head before he's even finished speaking. "Whatever you need to say to me is four years too late."

He rears back like I've slapped him and the hurt that crosses his beautiful face almost makes me want to apologize, but I don't. Not this time. Maybe not ever again.

"I think I might have a solution to the Calm Monitor," he blurts out.

That gets my attention. He knows just how to reel me in. I'm so desperate to find a way out of this situation, to find a solution, that I go along with it. I stare at him for a moment, everything inside me warring against believing him, believing in him again. Not after he walked away with nothing more than a bullshit excuse.

But still, I nod, unable to form words around the knot in my throat, and we get to work.

Over the next half hour, we stack furniture onto crates and blocks. Move anything from the floors. Put down plastic tarps over larger furniture. We move quickly and efficiently, using the comfortable shorthand that we developed when we first started working together years ago. It feels familiar. After we've protected as much as we can from the water that continues to flood in, Knox finds the circuit board and turns the power off. I stand in the foyer, taking one last look at my home as the lights go out. He comes to join me and we stand there quietly in the dimly lit room for a moment.

"Thank you," I say, my voice barely a whisper.

"You're welcome. Let's get out of here."

"You can just drop me at a hotel," I say, digging my feet in.

"I'm not dropping you at a hotel. You'll be more comfortable at my place and you know it." He takes my bag from my hands and walks out the door into the torrential downpour toward his car.

Once he's put my bag in the back seat, he turns to me as I slowly follow him out. His hood is pulled up over his head so I can barely make out his face, but I can see the determination in his stance.

I'm too tired to fight him right now. The whole ordeal has been exhausting. The flood of emotions I feel seeing him for the first time in four years nearly knocks the breath right out of me. There's an ache in my chest I refuse to believe is a signal that I've been missing him. It's just the residue of panic from seeing my home flooding.

The rain continues to beat down. The force of the wind whips hard raindrops sideways across my face. I pull up the hood on my rain jacket and slowly make my way down the steps toward him.

"I suggest you cancel that rideshare before it gets here. Would hate for your rating to go down." He smiles softly at me. He folds his arms and leans on the car. He's waiting. Waiting for me so patiently. Like he always has. Waiting for me to catch up. Or, better yet, for my brain to catch up with my feelings.

I shake my head and look away from his beautiful golden face. He's one of the few people I could stare at forever. There's so much familiarity there, it's almost too hard to look at.

His body tenses like he can sense me preparing to run

away, and he's not wrong. Everything in me wants to hightail it out of here. Storm be damned. "Renee, you can be pissed at me. You don't even have to speak to me. But I need you to let me help you. Let me keep you safe. Now get in the car," he says firmly.

"Where are you taking me?"

"To my place." My eyebrows shoot up. Then he quickly adds, "Just until Jordyn is back." I'm practically gripping my sides to keep from falling apart. My face is slick with rain. The cotton sweatpants I slept in are beginning to stick to my skin, heavy and wet. A combination of sensations I do not like.

Knox slowly moves toward me and wraps his arms around me tightly, the way I've always liked. I instantly start to feel relief even though I don't want his comfort. I squeeze my eyes shut and breathe him in. He holds me and starts to sway a little. The rocking motion, being wrapped firmly in his arms, feels like I'm under a weighted blanket in a hammock. It's so grounding, I don't want it to end.

Speaking softly in my ear, he says, "Come on, Nay. Let's go home."

He moves backward toward the car, still holding me. I hear the door open. "I'm going put you in the car now. You don't have to open your eyes if you don't want to. I'll help you in." Knox has always known how to take care of me when I've become so overwhelmed that I just shut down. I hate that he still remembers what I need all these years later.

Gently, he helps me get into the car, careful of my head, and buckles me in. I lean back in the seat and only open my eyes when he gets in the car on the driver's side. When I turn to him, I wish I hadn't. He's staring at me like he's reacquainting himself with my face, then breathes a shuddering breath before speaking. "Okay, time to go. We'll be home in about fifteen minutes."

I stare out the windows and don't even bother to try to

process what just happened. All I know is that I feel safe for the first time in days. That despite everything that has happened between us, I still feel safest when I'm with Knox.

One thing at a time.

I can spend time processing what that means another day.

Chapter 6

RENEE

HOURS LATER, I wake up in Knox's massive penthouse apartment. The walls must be thickly insulated because I only barely hear Knox moving around the apartment. I'm not sure what time it is. By the time we finally made it back to his place, I was exhausted. He showed me to the guest bedroom and I collapsed onto the bed barely pausing to remove my soaked clothing. I was asleep before my head hit the pillow.

I lie in bed, trying to decide what to do now. Do I go out and talk to him? Do I hide in this room that could fit my bedroom twice over?

I'm no closer to making a decision when I hear a soft knock on the door. "Yes," I answer, voice husky with disuse. Knox opens the door just enough to poke his head in.

"Hey, you're awake. Good." His soft, rumbling voice and smile make me squirm a bit. I pull the covers up around me like they will protect me from his undeniable charm.

I hate that I missed his face. I don't want to be reminded of that right now when I need to be figuring out the repairs to my house. "I made a late lunch. I figured you'd be hungry when you woke up. Why don't you come on out and eat something?" I can tell by the slight smirk on his full lips that he knows I was thinking about hiding in this room forever.

"Yeah, okay. I'll be out in a minute." I try to appear unaffected, almost bored, by the prospect of being in the same room with him, but I feel like there's a hive of bees working their way up my limbs to my chest. My mind swirls with questions. Does he know what his company has done? Was he part of it? I'm not sure I'm ready to know the truth. I'm not ready to lose the last scrap of respect I have for him.

I quickly dress and head into the en suite bathroom to splash some cool water on my face. I stare at myself in the mirror and do some breathing exercises to try to calm myself before I leave the room to face him.

Knox is in the kitchen and whatever he's cooking smells heavenly. My mouth waters and my stomach tightens with hunger. I walk over to sit on a stool at the kitchen island. He places a cool glass of water before me that I gulp down immediately to clear the dryness from my throat. As I sip and he cooks, I look around the space, finally taking in his massive apartment—or penthouse, I guess. It's not the type of place I would have ever expected Knox to live but does seem fitting for the CEO of a major corporation. Cold, corporate, with ultra-modern, sleek monochrome grey furniture. One whole wall is just an expanse of floor-to-ceiling windows with a view of the capital and Austin's busy downtown.

The sky is still grey and heavy, but the rain has receded. Knox stands in the kitchen with his back to me, separated by the white marble kitchen island that extends all the way to the end of the kitchen. I start to picture all the dinner parties he's probably hosted here, the room filled with his new friends and fans celebrating his life as the youngest CEO in our industry. Parties at which I would never fit in. A life we would have never had together if he had stayed.

Before I know it, there's a bowl of chili in front of me, topped with sour cream, cheese, and corn chips. I dig in immediately. One good thing about Knox is he knows how to make a mean chili. He joins me at the kitchen island and we eat in silence. The only sounds are spoons scraping the bowl and cups clinking against the marble island as we sip our drinks. The moment helps to settle my nerves. It also makes me nostalgic for all the times we spent together just like this. Knox is one of the few people with whom I can be in comfortable silence.

When we were starting Renox, we'd spend hours working alongside each other, focused on our work, without saying a word. It never felt weird or awkward. I never felt alone when I was with him. The reminder makes me sad and that sadness makes me want to break the silence.

"Jordyn should be back later tonight. I'm going to stay with her until it's safe to go back to my house." I say all this in a quick rush, never taking my eyes off my bowl.

Knox chews his food and listens to me speak. "I think you should just stay here."

"Knox, no."

"Hear me out." He looks at me seriously. I shake my head. But he goes on anyway.

That makes me snap. How dare he ask me to hear him out? Where was his explanation when he just up and walked away from our company? And how can he ask me to stay after what his company has done?

"No, Knox. I won't hear you out. I don't trust you and I don't know that I ever will again. Not after…" I can't even say the words. It hurts too much.

"Renee, just give me a chance to explain what happened,

and then if you still want to leave, I'll take you anywhere you want to go."

"Which part will you explain? The part where you abandoned me and the company we started together? Or the part where LyonTech used me?"

Knox shakes his head, hands held up in surrender. "Renee, please. I didn't even know that Renox had any business with LyonTech. I've only been CEO for a few months. I barely have a handle on things. But I will find a way to fix this."

Reading people's body language and facial expressions has never been easy for me. But I know Knox better than I know anyone else except my mom. At this moment, I can feel his sincerity, even if it's not easy to accept.

I sigh and shake my head. It feels like there is so much unsaid. We used to be so good at talking to each other. So good at showing up for each other. And then that all ended and I still don't know why.

I stare down at my hands on the cool marble countertop to steady myself.

"Why, Knox? Why did you leave me?" It comes out as a whisper because even saying the words kicks the air right out of my lungs. Lately, I've been feeling like I'm always in a state of overwhelm. My body feels flooded with stress all the time. Managing a business on my own, seeing my work being used in unethical ways, and realizing that I handed LyonTech the blueprint to do it. Now my ex-best friend is sitting right next to me, another reminder of a situation that I failed to properly read. How did I not see it coming? How did I not see any of this coming and how can I ever trust myself again?

I feel Knox's eyes on me. I shift my eyes in his direction, and I'm stunned by the look of pure misery on his face.

"Renee, I'm so sorry. I never wanted to hurt you, but he…" Knox takes a breath and gathers himself. "It was Dad. He called me and told me he was dying. He asked me for my help and I … I couldn't say no."

"I'm so sorry," I say, not sure what else to say. The day he told me he was leaving to go work at his father's company, it was like a bucket of ice-cold water was dumped on me. We were just getting off the ground. We had just successfully landed our first client—and then he was gone. He tried to convince me that his going to work for LyonTech was a good thing and that he could find ways to partner with Renox. He even suggested that Renox could become a subsidiary of the larger firm. I shut him down. I felt betrayed and there was no way I was going to work for LyonTech. Why didn't he tell me the truth back then?

When I finally did decide to sell them my patent, it was a desperate attempt at trying to save the company after way too many months of losing contracts to larger firms.

Knox continues, "He didn't want anyone to know that he was sick so he made me sign an NDA and promise that I wouldn't share the information with anyone until he was ready. Corporate governance is cutthroat. He was convinced that the moment he announced that he was sick, he would be pushed out. He wanted to control the succession process."

Everything he's saying to me makes sense, yet I feel no less heartbroken. I get it; that is who Knox is. He's someone who will sacrifice anything for the people he loves and, in the end, he sacrificed our friendship and our business for his family. It hurts but I understand it. He'll probably never choose me and that's okay. I can live with that. But I won't let his company take my integrity, my belief, in what is right and just.

"Did you know that LyonTech was going to turn my biometric design into a tool of punishment and control?"

The way his eyebrows shoot up, I can't tell if he's surprised that I know what they're up to or if he really has no idea what they're about to do.

"I sold my design to LyonTech a year ago. Three months ago, I learned that instead of using my biometric system the way it was intended, they've altered the design—"

He shakes his head, cutting me off. "That's not uncommon. We buy patents all the time and make adjustments so they have a better shot at making it to market."

"It's wrong. What they're doing is completely wrong and unethical and will cause so much harm." I can't believe he doesn't see that. How can he justify what his company is doing?

"Renee, I know that your designs are personal to you. I can totally see how it must have been difficult to see your work edited, but this is business."

I shake my head and take another look around the sterile apartment to confirm just how much he has changed before I finally turn to face him. "Business? This is about more than business. This is people's lives. That biometric system could have improved the lives of millions of nonspeaking disabled people." In fact, it's designed to detect and reduce distress and prevent the use of more punitive and invasive measures like restraints. "But instead, LyonTech is selling my biometric monitor system to Caldwell Homes, a corporation that runs residential treatment facilities known for their abuse. Is that what you signed up to do as CEO of LyonTech? Profit off the abuse? I had my doubts about selling to a corporation like LyonTech, but I felt certain it would be the best way to make sure this technology reached the people who needed it. The only reason I trusted them was because of you. Because you were there, and I thought ... I thought, despite everything that happened between us, that I could still at least trust you to do the right thing."

Knox nods, taking in what I'm saying, and stands to face me. I hadn't even realized that amid my rant, I stood up and started pacing back in forth. But I said what I needed to say.

The question is, does he hear me? Does he see how wrong this is?

"Knox, I have to fix this. I can't…"

"Let me help you. I'll look into it. It hasn't gone into production yet so there's still time to roll back the changes and make some amendments to the contract with Caldwell to prevent misuse."

I look at him—really look at the man who used to be my friend, and wonder if I can trust him again.

He continues, his voice a little softer, "In the meantime, I think you should stay here until your house is fixed. We can work on getting the Calm Monitor back on track and maybe we can find a way to be friends again. Just give me a couple of weeks. Please, Renee. Let me fix this thing with LyonTech and … maybe our friendship?"

"Let me think about it." I take my plate to the kitchen sink and pour myself some more coffee.

"Okay." Knox nods, seeming satisfied with that response. He follows me into the kitchen, taking the plate from me, then brushes by me to the dishwasher. We barely touch but being this close to him makes me need to breathe more deeply and I quickly move out of his way and head back into the guest bedroom. Before I make it back to the room, he calls to me.

"Renee, I'm really glad you're here. I've missed you so much."

I nod, unable to find words around the knot forming in my throat, then head into the room and close the door. It's only once the door is closed that I let out a gasp. I sit on the edge of the bed, rocking back and forth. I can feel the flood of anxiety in every muscle, and heat blossoming in my stomach. I never felt the need to hide from Knox, but for some reason, I don't want him to know how much I'm struggling. How much I've been struggling for months. He would just try to comfort me and the thought of being comforted by someone who could just up and leave at any moment makes me feel desperate and vulnerable in a way I never want to feel again. Because if he walks away again, I don't know that I'll recover.

Chapter 7

KNOX

MONDAY MORNING, Renee is still at my house. She hid in the guest bedroom all day Sunday, only sneaking out to grab food from the kitchen before returning to the room. As much as I wanted to push my way past all her barriers, I knew she had a lot to process and needed her space.

The good news is the furor on social media seems to have died down. I've had my PR department monitoring the issue, tracking mentions of Renee, Renox, and LyonTech for the past few days. But that doesn't mean the problem has resolved itself. Activists were still parked outside our offices on Friday and the entire uproar has sparked a conversation about ethical tech, online and on cable news. I've gotten half a dozen calls asking me to comment on articles being written, and half a dozen more requests for interviews with prime-time news shows. I can only imagine that Renee is feeling the pressure too. I can imagine, but I don't know for sure because she has yet to face me again since lunch on Saturday.

Seeing her again made me realize just how much I've missed her. She's just as stunning as I remember, even standing in her house with water up to her ankles, wearing baggy sweatpants and an old T-shirt, her curly brown hair pulled up on top of her head. Corkscrew strands falling free down her neck. I remember watching her push away those strands from her neck on days when she was feeling extra fidgety and couldn't stand the feel of her own hair. I'd grab one of her headbands and toss it to her so she could finally end what seemed like constant frustration. Those were the kinds of things I would always notice about her when we were friends. Now I'm noticing that her hips are a little fuller and her delectable lips look as if she nervously bites them. Her smooth brown skin makes me want to press my nose right into her neck and breathe her in. Does she still smell like citrus?

I thought that with enough space and time, I would get over my feelings for Renee. But I'm beginning to realize that's not the case at all.

I'm already dressed for work, drinking my coffee at the kitchen counter, when Renee finally comes out of her room. "Good morning," she offers softly, breaking the silence that seems to have permeated the entire space since we last spoke more than a day ago.

"Good mornin'." I turn and smile at her over my coffee mug. "Can I get ya some coffee or breakfast?"

"I got it." She heads into the kitchen and grabs the mug I sat on the counter for her, next to the coffeepot. After she's prepared her own mug, she turns to face me, leaning her back against the counter. She takes a long sip before finally lifting her long lashes, revealing those gorgeous brown eyes. "I got the call."

I nod. I asked my assistant Martin to call her and invite her to come to the LyonTech offices this morning for a strategy meeting to discuss a plan to address the controversy around the

Calm Monitor. Given how tense things were between us, I figured it would be better if a neutral third party made the invitation.

"It's no longer trending on social media, but we still need to come up with a plan. These things have a way of spiraling out of control if you don't address them head on."

She nods and listens, eyes downcast again, staring off at something I can't see. My fingers itch to lift her chin and make her come back to me from where her thoughts have drifted. After a pause, she says, "I never thought my work would be called into question like this." She releases a long breath and then looks up at me. It's only then that I truly see the toll this has taken on her. Renee is usually excellent at concealing her feelings, even from herself at times. But right now, I see the pain, the shame, the confusion all swirling in her brown eyes. Her full lips turned down in a slight pout; the dark circles under her eyes are probably from spending hours scrolling, researching, and reviewing her own design plans to figure out what went wrong.

I get up from my seat and move around the counter to be closer to her, resisting every instinct to pull her into my arms and try to wash away her pain. "We're going to figure this out. You're an amazing designer. No one cares about creating inclusive disability tech as much as you. The fact that you're caught up in this storm is on us. But we're going to work it out and minimize the blowback on you going forward. I wasn't involved in the original deal, but I will personally see to it that we fix this." I finally move to her, placing my hands on her shoulders firmly. "Renee, I never meant to hurt you. Not back then and certainly not now. I will fix this, no matter what it takes, but I need you to work with me to make it happen."

She looks at me searchingly, as if she can't quite decide whether to believe me. The fact that she even has to pause guts me. She used to trust me unquestioningly. But I only have myself to blame for where we are right now. I'll do whatever it takes to prove that she can trust me again. Just having her here in my space, even barely speaking to me—knowing that she's here has settled something inside of me that I didn't realize was missing. I don't want to lose her again. But if I don't find a way to fix this, I just might.

After a quick detour back to Renee's house to survey the damage and grab some more clothes, we head to LyonTech. The glass-front tower rises before us. Renee stares at it with a frown and, for a moment, I see it through her eyes. Grandiose, imposing, a symbol of the corporate tech world. A world she's worked hard to avoid. Yet here we are.

"I know. It's a lot." I laugh, shaking my head. My charcoal grey suit fits perfectly with this environment. Renee is dressed in tailored joggers, white tennis shoes, and a sweater that leans into her curves perfectly.

Her buoyant brown curls with hints of honey highlights catch the sun, framing her almond-shaped face. Big hair, with an even bigger brain inside that beautiful head of hers. "Come on. We have a few minutes before the meeting starts—let me show you around." For some reason, I really want her to like it. I don't know why. It's not like I'd ever convince her to come work here. Tried that. Failed. Over the last four years, I've put a lot of work into transforming LyonTech into a modern workplace. More open space. Greenery. A range of different spaces designed to spark creativity. Gone are the grey cubicles and austere conference rooms. There's natural light, color, a mix of private offices and open workstations with standing desks, and a mix of seating to accommodate everybody's needs. Long before I became CEO, I was given free rein to turn it into the kind of workplace that young people like me—and hopefully Renee—would want to work in.

As we walk through the dining hall with its indoor and outdoor balcony seating, and a food court with every type of cuisine you could want, LyonTech employees gather at comfy restaurant-style seating, chatting and enjoying their meals. The space inspires easy connection, collaboration, and camaraderie. Renee looks around, taking it all in. Her expression gives nothing away. Damn, I really want her to like it.

"This is all you, isn't it?" she says.

I nod and smile. "Yeah," I say proudly. "Remember that summer before senior year when we interned here?"

Finally, she smiles. "God, I hated it. It was so grey, cold, and quiet."

How could anyone create in an environment like that? "We turned an empty office into our own creative design studio. Covered the walls in images to create a huge mood board and spent three months dreaming up our own ideas."

A laugh bursts out of her that fills me with light. "If you weren't the boss's son, we would have been fired. We never did any of the work we were supposed to do." She shakes her head with a rueful smile curving her soft lips. Just as quickly, it melts away.

"That was the summer we decided to start Renox Tech. So we wouldn't end up working in a place like that." Her words are loaded with the same sense of loss that I feel for our company, our friendship.

I wonder if she spent as much time as me thinking about what could have been. If I had stayed. If he hadn't called. Thinking of my father makes something sharp press against my chest. But before I can get sucked down too far under that weight, Renee brings me back.

"You did good, Knox. I'm really proud of you." Those words mean more to me than she could ever know.

We make our way up to the conference room with five minutes to spare before my team begins filing in. It's only when the room is filled with PR, legal, and my CFO Jeffrey that I realize I should have encouraged Renee to bring her own team in. She's outnumbered. But she doesn't seem intimidated by the space, and that's something I've always loved about Renee: no matter where she is, no matter the room, she stands fully in her power—or, at least, it looks that way on the surface.

I watch her from the corner of my eye as she sits next to me. I notice the repetitive movement of her fingers hidden in her lap and those protective instincts flare to life again. If we weren't surrounded by six other people, I'd want to put my own hands to work soothing her. Wrap her in my arms until she feels grounded, safe again.

I put those thoughts aside, trusting that Renee is more than capable of taking care of herself. Then I start the meeting. I turn to my head of PR. "Jason, why don't you kick us off?"

"Of course." Jason turns toward the TV screen and begins walking us through a series of social-media analytics. "As you can see, mentions of all involved have died down considerably over the last forty-eight hours. Just as we suspected." He pushes his thick black glasses up his nose and clears his throat before continuing. "But we expect that there will be another wave coming soon. The activist group..." He looks down to check his notes. "Autistics United is planning a major action outside one of Caldwell's facilities soon and ... more concerning is the, uh, petition going around demanding that LyonTech end the contract with Caldwell."

Fuck. I had a feeling something like that was coming. "Is it gaining any traction?" I ask.

"Three thousand signatures so far and growing," Jason soberly confirms.

Jeffrey slaps his hand down on the table. "This is ridiculous. We are not going to capitulate to some people on the internet signing their name. Most of them probably didn't read the petition before signing it. Caldwell is our largest client. This contract is worth nearly eighty million dollars. If we start making business decisions based on the whims of the woke mob on the internet, we'll be out of business in no time."

I keep glancing at Renee, wondering when she's going to say something. Anything. Her silence is completely unnerving me right now. This is her design; surely she has something to say about how it's used.

"I have a suggestion," Jason cuts in. I nod at him to continue. "Given your history." He gestures between Renee and me. "You started an edutech firm together five years ago and went to college together. If the two of you worked together on addressing some of the issues that have been named—not to mention, Renee, you are the perfect person to speak about the value of this product. I understand that you yourself are ... uh ... someone with the uh ... the uh ... issues that the Calm Monitor is designed to address. I think you could—" As Jason fumbles with his words, Renee shrinks beside me, the movement of her hand increasing in pace.

I put up my hand. "Jason, let me stop you right there. I'm not going to speak for Renee. She's more than capable of doing that herself—and explaining to you what's problematic about what you're trying and failing to say. But what I will say, as CEO of this company, is that I will not put her in a position to be tokenized and used to give credibility to this company. That's not how we do business." I level back firmly.

Renee finally leans forward, placing her hands on the table. Appearing calm as ever. She looks around the room before speaking. "I think what you were trying to say is that I'm autistic. But no, I will not use my experience to convince the public to trust LyonTech or the Calm Monitor. I'll prove that it's safe and effective and can't be used to cause harm. But I think LyonTech needs to think long and hard about the types of companies you do business with." Then she looks at me. "Do you really want your name associated with a place like Caldwell? Have you seen the videos of what happens in that place?

The Calm Monitor was never meant to be in the hands of a company like Caldwell." She pauses. "But if you insist on selling to them, then I want to revise the blueprint to prevent misuse."

I nod, not even bothering to look toward Jeffrey, who I'm sure is practically foaming at the mouth. Renee looks at me searchingly, shakes her head, and sighs before finishing. "And if working with Knox is what it takes to do that, then that's what I'll do." I can barely hold back the smile. Here's my shot. My one shot at a second chance with Renee.

Chapter 8

KNOX

AFTER THE MEETING, we ride the elevator down to the parking garage to exit the LyonTech offices. Renee and I stand side by side, silently watching the elevator descend floor by floor. My mind keeps wandering back to the meeting, to her challenge to me about being associated with Caldwell.

When we reach the bottom, I feel a tiny bit of relief that the elevator made no stops and no one got on to join us. The cool air in the garage blankets me with a jolt, followed by a shocking flash of light to my left. I quickly turn to see a man, face covered by a camera, taking pictures of me.

"Ms. Johnson, do you care to comment on the controversy over your Calm Monitor? Did you know it would be sold to Caldwell when you sold your patent to LyonTech?"

What the fuck?

Renee is frozen in place, trying to gather herself enough to speak. I press my hand to the middle of her back and firmly push her forward. We are not doing this today.

I angle my body toward the flash of the camera and guide us to my car. I focus on getting Renee into the car only a few feet away, but it may as well be a hundred-yard dash to get there. The photographer matches us step for step, shooting questions at us, as I hustle Renee to the car. As I open the car door, he gets a little too close and I turn on him. "Hey! Back up —now!" I growl at him and he immediately takes a step back, but the cocky grin on his face makes me want to knock him on his ass.

Once Renee is in the car, I look her over to make sure she's okay. She looks shell-shocked. "Hang on, we'll be out of here in a minute," I say.

I shut her door and begin walking around the driver's side, never taking my eyes off him.

"You're trespassing. You need to leave now," I yell at him. Then I jump in the driver's seat of my Jeep.

I speed out of LyonTech's underground parking garage like we're being chased by paparazzi. The whole time, I keep sneaking looks at Renee to make sure she's all right. "Breathe, Nay," I say softly. She's staring straight ahead, eyes trained on the road ahead, but I can tell she's in her head somewhere. Her entire body is tense, fingers digging into her hands. My own hands grip the steering wheel, desperate to touch her. To soothe away her tension. It's like there's a tether between our bodies. I can just sense when she's anxious and overwhelmed, no matter how hard she tries to hide it. I can see beneath the masks she presents to the world. Or, at least, I used to be able to.

"I'm fine," she sighs, sinking back into the seat and flexing her fingers open. "I just wasn't expecting there to be press. This is just…" She breaks off, but I don't even need her to finish to know. It's just all too much. How did one product, one contract, turn into this controversial uproar?

Renee has never wanted to be in the spotlight. She's always

loved her work. Loved what she does. When we first started Renox, we made a deal. I would be the public face of the company, the salesman pitching our ideas to potential clients, and she would be more behind-the-scenes, project-managing our product launches. That wasn't my idea. I wanted us to both be the face, but Renee hated the kind of song and dance that was needed to sell our ideas, and it always came more naturally to me. In fact, if I'm honest, I thrive on it. I love talking to people, finding out what their pain points are, and pitching them an idea that they'll instantly fall in love with. Maybe it's why my dad chose me to become the next CEO of LyonTech. I'm a born salesman. But if I was the charismatic face of our company, Renee was the true heart and soul. She was the North Star, keeping us aligned with our mission and vision for the ways in which technology could improve the lives of children, families, and adults with disabilities.

She was my North Star until … I left. It's only in the last few days, having her back in my life, that I've truly felt how deeply I've missed her. I've missed my Nay. But something feels different between us. I know it's been a while since we've spent time together. Years have stretched out between us and so much has happened in both of our lives. She's the same, yet not quite the same woman that I became friends with in college, the woman who became my closest friend, my business partner. She's different. A bit more closed off than I remember. Or maybe it's just me. Maybe she's closed herself off to me. After what I've done, I'm not sure I can blame her, but if we have any shot at saving both of our reputations, then we have to work together to find a solution to the Calm Monitor.

We pull into my parking spot in my building's garage. I turn off the ignition and then turn to look at her to make sure she's really okay. She turns to look at me.

She must read the question in my mind. "Really, I'm fine." But she has a weary look on her face. We silently ride the elevator up to my penthouse. Seconds after we exit into my living room, the elevator doors close behind us and my phone beeps with a notification. Renee continues into the room, flopping down on the couch as I stop in the middle of the living room to pull out my phone. What I see makes any warmth drain out of my body.

"How the fuck…" I start.

Renee immediately jumps back up from the couch. "What?" She walks over to me. "What is it now?"

I show her the picture of the two of us and the caption that is already racking up reposts, and comments, for some online publication called *TappedIn*. The photographer outside my office must have posted it as soon as we pulled away. It's a picture of me and Renee in the parking garage, my hand protectively pressed to her back—her shoulders hunched forward and head down—while holding up my other hand aggressively toward the photographer with a scowl on my face. The caption reads: *LyonTech's CEO and the creator of the Calm Monitor seems to be in bed together in more ways than we think.*

"Oh, my God," Renee gasps. "This just keeps getting worse. Now it looks like we're fucking. Like I'm some fragile, vulnerable fool who needs you to take care of me."

My eyebrows shoot up because I don't think I've ever heard Renee use the word "fuck" before and I feel a little tingle in the base of my spine just hearing that word come out of her mouth. That tingle completely dies, though, when I see her roll her eyes at the thought.

Well, damn.

"Okay, we need to sort this out ASAP before rumors start flying around about us," Renee says. "It's only a matter of time before they figure out that we used to be business partners and that you co-founded Renox. They'll start to twist this story even more and make it look like we're engaged in some shady backroom deals. This situation has already caused enough damage.

Renox can't afford a hit like this. We're already … never mind. I just need this to end now."

Renee paces the room.

"Wait, what's going on with Renox?"

She looks at me and the look of pain and fire in her eyes nearly makes me take a step back. "That's none of your concern anymore. The point is we need to fix this now," she says, turning to face me. Yeah, definitely not the old Renee. This Renee has a fire to her that I've never seen before. It's like she burned away the fragile edges and replaced them with a sharper, more focused version of herself.

"So here's what's going to happen," she continues. "I will stay here at your place for the next few weeks until my house repairs are done. You and I will work at finding a way out of this situation with the Calm Monitor, and then we'll go our separate ways again. Got it?"

I swallow hard, utterly confused by the tumultuous mix of feelings inside me right now. The Caldwell deal is a problem for both of us, for different reasons, and solving it is in both our best interests, but the thought of that being the end of us just doesn't sit right with me.

"I'm sure we can find a mutually beneficial solution," I say. But I'm hoping that it won't mean the end of us. That's the part that I don't say.

Chapter 9

KNOX

I SPEND the rest of the day working from home, hoping to avoid any more run-ins with reporters. Renee hides in the guest bedroom, probably working as well. We've agreed to take a break and regroup and discuss strategy over dinner.

Every time I walk past the hallway and into the kitchen to refill my coffee mug, I glance at the door, hoping she might pop her head out or walk down the hall. Any excuse to cross paths with her.

Her words still echo in my head, *fragile, vulnerable fool who needs you to take care of me.* Since when does she care what other people think of her, of us, and our relationship?

But I can't deny that it all looks bad, and if this reporter or any other social-media sleuth decides to dig, they will find out that we have a long history together. Not for the first time, it makes me wonder who was involved in the deal with Renox, and why wasn't I told about it? I have my assistant, Martin, doing some digging to find out. Something about it just doesn't feel right. I've been at LyonTech for four years; there's no way they didn't know about my connection to Renox when they decided to buy the Calm Monitor. Why wasn't I brought in on the negotiations, or at least informed that we'd bought her patent?

It's only when Renee's door begins to open that I realize that I've been standing at the end of the hallway, staring at her door with an empty coffee mug in hand. I practically dive into the kitchen before the door fully opens. Things are already awkward between us without me looking like a creeper standing outside her bedroom door.

I'm busy in the kitchen, about to pour what must be my fifth cup of coffee, when I hear her behind me. "Hey, I have a couple of things to grab from my place. I'll be back in a few hours."

I put down the mug and turn around. "I'll give you a ride."

"No," she says, stopping me in my tracks.

"Are you sure?"

"Yes, I need to pick up my car anyway and … I just need some space."

I nod and toss my car keys back onto the kitchen counter. "Got it." She needs her space. I need to respect that, even if it sucks. I need to move at her pace. I'm the one who walked away. I don't just get to demand that things go back to the way they once were between us. If I want a shot at repairing my relationship with Renee, I need to be patient.

Instead, I start working on dinner.

By the time Renee returns an hour later, I've prepared a chicken stir fry and set the table for two. She walks in, arms loaded down with bags and camping supplies. I raise an eyebrow at the hiking pack she slides off the elevator with her foot.

"What's all this?" I ask, coming to help her with her bags.

"You decide you'd rather camp out than spend another night with me?"

"No, I'm leading a beginner overnight camping trip this weekend," she says, barely looking at me as she lugs her bags back to the room.

I pick up the pack from the floor and follow her. "Since when do you lead camping trips?"

"It's something I started two years ago. It's a volunteer program where experienced campers guide people new to outdoor experiences." She drops her bags on the chair next to the bed. I look around the room, the neatly organized room, and smile. Renee has always been super organized. A stack of books sits on the bedside table. Her laptop and journal are positioned perfectly on the desktop. The bed is neatly made, with not a wrinkle in sight. If I walk into the bathroom, I'm sure it will be just as immaculate. It's just so Renee. And even though she stands right in front of me, it makes me miss her even more.

Her phone rings and she answers, "Hey, Andy. I was actually just about to text you. We should go over the agenda for this weekend and make sure we have everything." She turns her back to me as she talks to who I assume to be her camping group co-leader.

I watch her closely. For a moment, my mind wanders to the camping trips we used to take together. We've backpacked most of the Southwest's best trails. Hours spent walking red dust trails. Renee in front. Me just behind, watching her every step. Sharing a tent and talking late into the night about our dreams for the future, about the business we would build together.

The nervous tone of her voice shakes me out of the memory. "What? Oh, no, Andy. I'm sorry to hear that. Yes, of course. I completely understand. No, don't worry about it. I can handle the group on my own. It's probably too last minute to find someone else but I'll try. Of course. Take care of yourself." She hangs up the phone and flops down on the bed.

"Is everything okay?" I ask, sitting down next to her.

"My co-lead, Andy, broke his leg. Now I either have to cancel the group or find someone else to fill in. We need at least two group leaders with a beginner group. Anything could go wrong."

"I'll do it," I say without hesitation. It's exactly what we need. To get out of this house. Be on the land with nothing but a pack and a map to guide us. This is my chance. A chance for us to reconnect and remember what it was like when we were friends.

"Knox, I don't think that's a good idea."

"Why not?" I ask.

She pauses for a moment, closing her eyes and shaking her head. "I know what you're trying to do. This used to be our thing. You think one night on a campsite, and we'll be us again." She turns to look at me and the hurt I see in her eyes makes me want to reach for her.

"Maybe it will never be like it was before," I admit. "We can't go back to the past. So much has changed for both of us. But that doesn't change the fact that we need to work together right now. Maybe this will help us clear the air. Because right now, you're avoiding me. Refusing to even look at me."

"It's not like that," she says, standing up, putting some space between us. "It's just … whenever I look at you, I remember how much it hurt when you left."

"Then you know how I feel," I say bitterly.

"What?"

"Renee, you left me before I left you. You moved out. Do you know how that felt? Having you pack up and move out of the apartment like that?"

She rears back, mouth falling open.

I jump up from the bed. "I'm going out for a bit. There's a stir fry on the stove."

"Knox, wait," she whispers.

"Look, think about it. Let me know if you want me to come. If not, we can just schedule a meeting at your office or mine and come to some agreement on how to manage this situation."

Then I throw on my running shoes, grab my keys, and head out before my emotions boil over and make things even more complicated than they already are.

An hour later, when I return from my run, I feel like the anger and hurt have drained from my body. But there's also a bit of shame left behind. I never want Renee to think that I left Renox to punish her for moving out, for not seeing how much her leaving hurt me. But if I'm honest with myself, maybe that was part of it, and acknowledging that makes me feel like shit. No wonder she doesn't want to be my friend anymore.

The lights are dimmed, the kitchen cleaned, and the food put away. On the kitchen counter is a sticky note. Written in Renee's looping handwriting is: *Let's go camping*. I smile, grab the note, and head to the bedroom, passing Renee's closed door on the way. For the first time, it doesn't feel like a rejection. I finally feel like I might have a chance to reconnect with the woman on the other side of that door.

Chapter 10

RENEE: *Five years ago*

A LIGHT SNOW falls overhead as I make my way down 5th Street toward the restaurant where I'm meeting Knox and his girlfriend, Val. It rarely snows in Austin but when it does, it has a dramatic effect on the city. The rare snowfall can bring the entire city to a standstill, but that doesn't stop Val from wanting tapas. I almost canceled on them. Did we really need to come out tonight? But since I've canceled the last two times we made plans, I felt like I need to show up. The overcast sky has turned the usually bright, vibrant earthy tones of the city into a depressing halo of grey. But the cold air smells clean and the light precipitation taps on my face lightly before melting against my skin. I like the feel of it. Growing up in California, I never got to see snow. I had to come all the way to the Southwest to experience it. I take quick, short steps like a waddling penguin, attempting to avoid falling on the slick ground beneath me.

    The rustle of my thick waterproof layers and the crunch of

the inch-thick layer underfoot fills my ears, nearly drowning out the sound of cars driving by and people chatting as they walk. It's a Saturday night and I guess everyone has agreed that a little bad weather won't stop them from enjoying their weekend.

I hate driving in this weather, mostly because other drivers become so much less predictable. Not everyone feels the need to slow down when the roads are slick. Luckily, Knox and Val chose a restaurant within walking distance of our apartment.

As the restaurant comes into view, I huff out a cold breath, preparing myself for a night of small talk. Val will pretend that she's interested in what Knox and I are working on before turning the conversation back to herself and her work as a social-media lifestyle influencer. I will sit quietly, nodding at all the right moments. Knox will attempt to pull me more into the conversation and find topics that Val and I might have a common interest in, but in the end, those attempts will fail and we'll end the night on an awkward note. I really don't know why he bothers. But for some reason, he's determined to make us friends. Tonight, I invited Jonathan to join us. He's just as chatty as Val and he'll take the pressure off me to talk.

As I approach the restaurant, I see Knox and Val sitting at a window seat. I stop just far enough away that they can't see me. He's so relaxed in his body. Broad shoulders leaning back against his chair. One hand casually resting on the table while he pushes a loose brown curl out of his eyes.

He's different with her. There's a lightness and playfulness that I don't see often. He sits back, casually gazing at her as she talks, an easy smirk on his full lips and amusement dancing in his eyes. I can imagine the familiar smell of sage on his light-brown skin. His head falls back as he laughs at something she's said. Then he responds with a wink before turning to check his phone. That's my cue.

Almost instantly, I get a text. *Almost here?* I quickly text back that I'm walking in now.

I walk into the restaurant, which is not as crowded as it would normally be on a Saturday. The weather did keep some people at home. I smile lightly at the hostess and point to my friends. She nods before turning back to her tablet to find a table for the couple that entered right behind me.

As soon as he sees me, Knox smiles and jumps out of his seat to greet me. He leans in close to speak into my ear, "Hey, I almost thought you weren't coming. I was going to head back over to the apartment to drag you out." I roll my eyes and nudge him away before turning to Val. Her strawberry blond waves fall in layers past her shoulders.

Despite the cold weather, she's wearing a form-fitting, spaghetti-strapped black dress that falls mid-thigh with boots that meet her hemline. The outfit shows off her Insta-model sexy looks. "Hey, girlie! I'm so glad you came out. How have you been? This sweater is so cute. Where did you get it? Where's your boyfriend? I can't wait to meet him."

My face is a frozen mask of pleasantry but underneath it, I'm working to tamp down the stirring feeling of overwhelm that always hits when people bombard me with a series of questions. Which am I supposed to answer first? Does she even want me to answer? Can I at least get settled first?

Knox comes to my rescue and places his arm around my shoulder. "Chill, Val. Give her a second to get settled first before you start pelleting her with questions." He guides me into the seat next to him. I catch Val's raised eyebrow at our seating arrangement but quickly turn my attention to the glass of water in front of me. I take a long sip to give myself a moment to regroup.

By the time I put the glass down, Jonathan is walking up to our table. "Hey, good people! I just saw someone bust their ass on the sidewalk outside. It's wild out there. People really don't know how to act in this weather." Knox doesn't bother to get up to greet him. Jonathan grabs the only remaining seat, next to Val, and they introduce themselves. Something about this whole dynamic feels slightly off but I can't figure out what it is.

We go through the motions of ordering drinks and then decide on some shared plates. Knox keeps leaning into me to look at the menu together, his arm draped around my chair. Val doesn't look particularly pleased by the gesture. I wonder if I should suggest we switch seats but that might make things even weirder.

I press the menu into his hands and grab the one in front of me. "You order whatever you want. I'll just get what I always get." I turn my attention to Jonathan before Knox can say anything more and ask him about his day. I try to ignore Knox as Jonathan talks about a new physical training client he just started working with who's an ultramarathoner. Eventually, I notice Knox pull back from my chair and turn to look at something on his phone. Jonathan starts showing us some video clips from his sessions that he's posted on Instagram, and before I know it, he and Val are comparing notes on follower numbers, content trends, and whatever else influencers discuss. I pretend to be interested but I've pretty much zoned out. That's when I feel Knox at my shoulder again.

"Renee?" I turn to look at him. "You okay? Say the word and we can call it a night and head home."

I know he's only trying to be helpful, but I feel a little annoyed by his question. "I'm fine. Just relax and enjoy the night. You don't need to be on babysitting duty."

That last comment sends his eyebrows cresting his scalp. "What?"

I take a deep breath and grab his knee under the table. "Let's talk about it later." The rest of the night passes in a blur. I know that when we get home, we'll have to talk about what I just said. I can feel Knox's tension. He doesn't say much or engage in the conversations that Jonathan and Val have pretty much dominated.

By the end of dinner, I'm both relieved that it's over and dreading going home with Knox, where he will most certainly want to talk. Knox tells Val that we have an early morning and so she can't stay over tonight. It's not exactly true. Our pitch meeting isn't until noon, but we do have a little more prep to do in the morning. Val pouts but accepts that there will be no sleepover tonight. She does, however, insist on walking back to our apartment to grab something she left in Knox's room. Jonathan doesn't even bother to ask about coming back to our place. We never have sleepovers. I just can't stand having to share a bed with anyone.

At three months, Jonathan is my longest relationship. I've only had one other sexual partner and I've never successfully shared a bed with either of them. I've tried but always end up lying awake, unable to fall asleep, too distracted by the sound of someone snoring in my ear or moving on the bed next to me.

When we get back to the apartment, Knox heads to the bathroom while Val gets the toiletry bag she left here. I'm sure it's full of overpriced skin-care products made in Sweden or with ingredients from some plant that can only be found in the Amazon. When she comes out, she finds me in the kitchen, loading the dishwasher with this morning's breakfast dishes. "You know, he's always going to want to take care of you. The question is, is that really fair to him? To have to always be worried about you and your … issues?" Her question unleashes a tornado of emotions within me and at its core is a white-hot shame that leaves me frozen in my spot staring at the plate I've been rinsing in the sink.

Before I can full process what has just happened, Knox is back. "Did you find what you were looking for?"

She throws her arms around him. "I did, babe. You sure you don't want me to stay the night?"

Knox slides out of her arms and opens the refrigerator door. "It's not a good night, Val. We have to work in the morning."

She huffs out a dramatic sigh, whipping her hair over her shoulder again. Knox doesn't catch the way she glances at me and rolls her eyes before storming out of the apartment. No sooner is the door closed behind her than he turns to me. "What's going on? What was the comment about babysitting? What the hell is that supposed to mean?"

"You realize that since we met sophomore year, we've barely spent any time apart. Even summer breaks, you'd come to Berkeley or I'd go to your parents' house."

"And? You're my best friend. We're also business partners. Of course we spend time together."

"I don't think Val likes it."

"Who fucking cares?"

"How are we supposed to be in relationships with people…"

"Fuck people! You're my person. No one else gets a say." Knox turns and walks away. I continue to load the dishwasher when I hear him come back in. "I'm sorry," he says softly. "I don't know why I got so upset. I guess I just … you are one of the most important people in my life and I don't want anyone to come between us, ever."

I turn to look at him. He means it. If he had it his way, we'd share this tiny apartment forever. But he would never get to have a real relationship. He'd always be worried about me. Too focused on me. I look around our apartment. Everything in its place the way I want it, need it, to be. The space organized around my needs.

I walk over to him, wrap my arms around his waist, and look up into his beautiful brown eyes. "You're my person, too.

But I gotta learn how to be a person who can stand on my own."

He tenses under my hold. "What are you saying, Renee?"

I release him and step back. "I think I should move out."

I'm not looking at his face when I say it. But his sharp intake of breath feels like a punch to my stomach. I immediately want to take the words back, but they're already out there. I'm putting some space between us. We have always moved as one entity since we became friends in school. He's always felt like the protective big brother I could depend on, but recently I noticed more. I've longed for his touch in a new way—a way I've never felt for Jonathan. It feels way too good to be close to him. And one day, he's going to turn his lightness and protective care on to someone else, someone he's truly in love with, and I need to get out of the way to let him do that.

A month later, I move out.

Chapter 11

RENEE

WE ARRIVE at Grelle State Park, a two-hour drive from Austin, on an overcast Saturday morning around seven. It's the perfect place for a beginner camping trip. There are easy to moderate trails to hike, lake access, fishing, swimming, and paddleboating.

The sky is a mass of heavy grey clouds, the temperature hovering around sixty-five degrees. In the summer, the campsite and trails would be packed, but on a cool October day, our group is one of only a few out here today.

After I register our group with the park ranger's office and get our passes, I join Knox on the back of his truck. He passes me a thermos of coffee and we sit quietly, looking out over the still waters of Lake Travis. I check the time; the campers are going to be arriving soon. Before they do, I clear my throat, square my shoulders, and turn to Knox. "Listen, I appreciate you helping out, but…"

"You're the leader here, Renee. I'm just your assistant. Tell me what to do and I'll do it. I promise I won't overstep," he says to me. I nod and take him at his word.

I slip on my bright-green camp leader vest and stand to greet the campers as they park and gather around our meeting spot. It's not like I'm new to leading teams, but still, my stomach tightens a little at having to do this on my own for the first time. Usually, Andy does most of the talking and I provide more one-on-one support to campers, helping them figure out how to set up their tents and safely move through the trails and answer their questions. But today it will have to be me. I take a deep breath, looking at Knox. He just nods at me.

"Good morning, folks. Gather around." My voice falters a bit, fading off at the end. The group of five barely looks up. They're huddled together, chatting excitedly and introducing themselves. My nervousness ramps, but I clear my throat and try again. This time, louder. Lifting my arm in the air for emphasis.

"Good morning!" Finally, they turn to me, see the green vest, and realize I'm the camp leader. "Let's circle up." They slowly move closer and I get a better look at the group. There are four women and one man, ranging in age from early twenties to fifties. I take a moment to think back to how Andy used to handle this first part.

"Hey, y'all, I'm Renee and I'll be your group leader for this trip. This is my friend, Knox, who will be assisting me over the next day. Let's go around and introduce ourselves. Share your name and why you decided to join this trip."

There's a momentary pause as they peer around at each other sheepishly. No one wants to be the first to speak.

Finally, the sole guy in the group speaks up. He's a white guy in his twenties who looks like he spends more time in front of a computer than in the outdoors. He pushes his glasses up on his face and tugs at his beanie, turning to the group. "I'll go first. I'm Devan. I recently moved to Dallas for work and my firm is hosting a team camping trip. I'm the only member of my team who has never been camping. I just don't want to look like it ... so, trying to get a little experience under my belt." He shrugs and steps back into the small group.

A young blonde, wearing fitted green cargo pants and a pink puffer jacket, goes next. "Good morning, folks. I'm Becca and, I don't know, I guess I always just wanted to try camping. So here I am." She flips her hair back, directing her smiles at Knox. I peek at Knox to see if he notices but his full attention seems to be on me.

We continue around the group. There are two Black women, Terry and Sam, in their 40s who have been best friends for more than twenty years and are dreaming of hiking the Appalachian Trail together one day. There's Martha, a widow who just turned sixty and promised her husband before he died that she wouldn't give up on life, so she made a list of new experiences she was going to have, and camping was one of them.

Their stories remind me of why I fell in love with camping and backpacking and why I want to help other people have this experience too. I started leading these trips after Knox left because I felt so lonely and hurt and only these trips helped me feel connected to other people and the land.

"I hope that by the time you head home tomorrow morning, you feel a deep sense of connection to the land that we're standing on and you feel more confident in your ability to plan your own camping trips with family and friends." I take a deep breath and pull away the clipboard I've been pressing to my chest like an anchor. I quickly run the list of activities, eager for the spotlight to no longer be on me.

The group waits patiently for me to give them their next direction. "Okay! Let's start setting up camp." We all grab our packs and begin walking to the camping site. I notice Becca looking around a little frantically. I also notice that her backpack is much smaller than everyone else's so there is no way she could be carrying a tent. "Everything okay, Becca?"

She smiles sheepishly at me. "Umm … we're staying in cabins or, like, one of those glamping tents where everything is included, right?"

I raise my eyebrows and give Knox a WTF look. "Did you get the packing list that was sent out when you signed up?" I ask.

She smiles painfully. "I mean … I glanced at it."

I'm completely at a loss. What would Andy do right now? My instinct is to just send her home and tell her to try again another day when the group all begins to chime in.

Martha says, "Oh, sweetie, don't worry I'm sure we can sort you out." Everyone else begins to nod and offers to pitch in to make sure Becca has everything she needs to get through the night.

The group has already started to bond. If I send her home now, it will totally kill the vibe. Knox looks at me and just shrugs and mouths, "It'll be fine." So I decide to let it go and hope I don't end up regretting it.

When we finally get through setting up tents, I give the group some free time to hang out by the lake or walk along one of the nearby trails. I walk around the campsite, doing one final inspection of everyone's tent to make sure they've got their ground cloth down, adequate sleep padding, and a rain fly above their tents to protect them from the rain. It's only once I've made the rounds that I notice that Becca isn't the only person who forgot to pack a tent.

I find Knox stacking some wood for the fire later. "Hey, Knox, where's your tent?"

He drops the bundle of logs in his arms on the ground and turns to me. He smiles, and I notice a little charcoal mixed with his signature cedar and sage smell. "I didn't bring a tent."

"What do you mean, you didn't bring a tent?" I ask.

"Renee, we always share a tent," he says like it's obvious.

"Um, you mean we used to share a tent when we used to go camping together. But that was then."

He moves to begin preparing the fire pit with charcoal and logs. "Well, I guess we'll be continuing that tradition since I did not pack a separate tent."

I stare at him with my mouth hanging open, unable to respond, when Terry, Sam, and Martha return from their hike. They're laughing and talking, and for a moment I appreciate the sight and forget about being annoyed at Knox.

"Did you enjoy your hike?" I ask, smiling at them.

"It was great." Sam beams back at me. "And you were right about the layers. Half a mile in, I was stripping out of my jacket and pullover."

The rest of the day goes by in a blur of preparing meals, paddleboating, playing games, and exploring the park. By the time the sun starts to set, everyone begins to settle in for the evening. I let Knox talk them through how to build a fire. I stand back and watch him. He's so relaxed talking with people. It never feels forced for him.

Unlike me.

The entire day, I've been extra aware of every word out of my mouth, every facial expression, every detail of this trip, constantly double-checking that I didn't forget something or someone. But everyone seems to be just having fun, enjoying themselves. I'm deep in my own thoughts, running through another mental checklist, when I feel Knox at my shoulder. "You're doing great. Everyone's having a great time. Just relax."

By the time the sun has set we've enjoyed a classic campsite dinner of bratwurst and baked beans. Everyone seems happy and full. I sit back quietly and watch them around the fire, their faces all tinted with a warm golden hue.

Knox and Becca are directly across from me. I watch the

natural, easy way they engage with each other, and not for the first time I wonder why Knox is still single—a fact I only know because Jordyn told me. Becca reminds me of his ex-girlfriend. The same fit, thin build; golden blond hair that falls in natural waves around her face; the ability to flirt and do that back-and-forth banter thing that always makes me feel like I'm in a high-stakes game of ping-pong.

Knox throws his head back in laughter at something she says and my heart seems to stutter. I desperately want to go hide in the tent and not feel like I'm lurking on the outer edge of yet another social group. But I'm the camp leader. I can't leave.

Devan drops down in the seat next to me with his notebook and pen out. The whole day, he has been taking copious notes about everything I've taught them today. "Hey, do you mind walking me through the steps to create an appropriate sleep system again? I want to make sure I'm not missing anything."

Sure thing, Devan.

I spend the next thirty minutes answering every detailed question he has. It's just the distraction that I need to keep me from imagining Becca and Knox falling in love and telling a story about how it all began with a camping trip where neither one of them thought to bring a tent.

By the time I've finished answering all of Devan's questions, the group seems ready to call it a night. Knox walks over to where Devan and I are sitting on a log and sits down on the other side of me. His body presses against mine and he wraps an arm around my waist. I look at him quizzically and then return my focus to Devan. "Any other questions?"

Devan looks over his notes "Hmm ... not right now. Maybe tomorrow."

I try to ignore the feel of Knox pressed up against me. "Okay..."

Devan doesn't move but neither does Knox and so, for an

awkward moment, I'm sitting between them on this piece of wood. I turn to Knox. "You good?"

He gives me a look I can't quite read. All I can see is the fire dancing in his eyes. I feel the heat coming off his body, replacing the chill in the air, and his finger rubbing against my hip. I'm tingling and melting, feeling almost intoxicated.

"Goodnight, Devan," Knox says, never taking his eyes off me.

Finally, Devan looks up from his notes and realizes he's an unwelcome third in this party on a log. "Uh, yup, goodnight," he says and scoots off to his tent.

"You ready for bed?" he says softly, and those words send a zing straight through my core.

I press my legs together to chase the sensation a bit. Across the fire, Becca is watching us, but when we make eye contact, she quickly looks down at her phone.

I turn back to Knox and all I can do is nod.

Knox leads me to our tent, my hand pressed into his. Just as we're about to head in, I snap out of it and remember that I'm responsible for five other people who need to be ready to spend their first night sleeping outdoors. "Wait, I need to check in with them and make sure they're all set for the night." I try to pull my hand away, but he holds on more firmly.

"Already talked them through it while you were answering Devan about the sleeping bag temperature ratings and moisture-wicking fabrics," he says somewhat cynically while dragging me into the tent.

"Goodnight, you two!" someone calls out and I feel the urge to run out and explain that nothing is happening. We're just friends. He would never see me that way. He's more likely to date someone like Becca than me. But Knox has already dropped the flap on my tent, closing us in.

It's only once we're inside that I realize just how small this tent is, and the air mattress that I packed is even smaller.

"I can't believe you didn't bring a tent," I huff, shaking my head.

But Knox does not seem at all bothered by the accommodations. He strips down to his base layers, a long-sleeve tee and sweatpants, and climbs inside his sleeping bag, waiting for me to join him.

Thank God he brought a sleeping bag.

I don't know how long we lie there, side by side, staring at the tent ceiling, until he finally speaks. "You smell the same."

I turn my head at his comment.

He chuckles. "I know that's a weird thing to say but it's true. You used to smell like citrus. You still do. For a long time, I would try to find that scent. I couldn't figure out what it was. It wasn't perfume. I know you don't like perfume. So I figured it had to be a body wash or a lotion. I remember going to drugstores and department stores searching for it. Eventually, I realized that I just missed you. I missed the smell of you." He turns on his side toward me and breathes me in, eyes closed, a small smile on his face. We're both quiet for a moment.

"Weirdo," I say, and then we both crack up laughing and it feels so good. Almost like we used to be. When we were friends.

I close my eyes and try to sleep. But the feel of him so close to me has all my senses on high alert. It's like I'm afraid that when I wake up, he'll be gone again.

His voice cuts through the darkness. "I know you're awake."

I sigh and say nothing. I feel his hand move across the air mattress, stopping just next to mine, our pinkies barely touching. "Nay, I'm sorry that I ever made you feel I didn't respect you or trust you. I know you're strong. I know you don't need me." The emotion in his voice makes me long to wrap my arms around him.

"But that's the thing ... I do need you. I always have. But you left, and I had no choice but to figure it out on my own."

My voice is barely audible. "And honestly ... it has been really hard running Renox on my own."

He's quiet for a moment, and I can almost feel the wheels turning, trying to figure out how to begin. He turns in his sleeping bag to face me.

"I never wanted to leave you. But at the time, I thought I didn't have a choice. My father was diagnosed with an aggressive form of lymphoma. Renox had just completed our first product launch when he came to me and told me he was dying and didn't know how long he had left. His final wish was to know that I would take over LyonTech and continue the family legacy. He was proud of what we were building with Renox and even suggested that it become a subsidiary of Lyon, but I knew you would never go for that."

At first, I dismiss that explanation, but then I remember how important it was to me to be independent and socially driven and I know he's right. I continue to stare at the ceiling of our tent.

"Why didn't you just tell me? I was completely blindsided. One day we're planning our strategy for the next three years and the next you tell me you've decided the start-up life isn't for you and you want to go to work for the family business. Which made no sense because you never wanted to work for your dad." I feel like there are tiny fireworks going off in my body; I need to move.

Knox continues to watch me, one arm tucked beneath his head, his long, sweatpants-covered legs stretched inside the sleeping bag. "My dad was hiding his illness. He didn't want anyone to know. He even made me sign a nondisclosure agreement. He was afraid the board would push him out before he could plan his succession and put me into place as the new CEO. I couldn't tell you. Or, at the time, I thought I couldn't tell you. I think at the time I was devastated about losing him and I felt like I owed it to him to keep his secret. I kept thinking

I needed to make up for all the time I wasted trying to prove I was good enough to stand on my own. More than anything, I just wanted more time with my dad." He sits up, zipping down his bag and drawing his long legs up to rest his hands on his knees. "But in the process, I betrayed you. You were the most important person in my life up until that moment when my father told me he was dying and instead of turning to you, I lied to protect him and I've regretted it every single day since."

We remain quiet in the darkness. I unzip my sleeping bag so I can sit up and let his words sink in. We turn to face each other, sitting knee to knee. The small, dark, enclosed space creates a cocoon around us.

"I'm so sorry, Nay." His voice cracks and, without thinking, without wanting to, I reach out for him. He grasps my hands and pulls me toward him. He wraps his arms around me and holds me close, cradling my head against his chest and breathing his sage and cedar scent.

"You left me." I cry.

My own emotions startle me and I try to pull away, but he holds on tighter. "I'll never leave you again." His words are too much.

Where do new promises fit when all that's left is broken space? Our friendship was like a solid vessel. It held me. It provided stability. When I lacked shape and form, it provided the very structure I needed to remember my own wholeness, and he took that from me. Yet right now, here he is, holding me together as the last four years come flooding out of me in tears and breath and moans. He holds me until I can breathe without gasping and gulping in air. Until I no longer feel like every nerve ending is threatening to explode. His strong arms wrap around me, pulling me close, and I can no longer resist the truth.

Knox has always been my home.

Chapter 12

RENEE

BY THE TIME we get back to Knox's place, it's already late afternoon. The setting sun casts shadows across his expansive living space from the floor-to-ceiling wall of windows.

The ride back to Austin felt like old times. We laughed and talked and reminisced. We sent Jordyn a few roadside selfies, knowing she would be happy to see us together again, and it really did feel like us again—the way we were before everything fell apart. I talked about the Calm Monitor and what inspired me to design it. I told him about wanting to find a way to help anyone trapped in a nonverbal state of distress, how many times I struggled to communicate my own anxiety and pain when I was in a complete state of shutdown.

He listened the way that he always did, and for the first time in a long time, I felt like I didn't have to explain myself to the point of exhaustion. With Knox, I never had to worry that he would try to downplay my experiences or try to come up with an oversimplified solution that dismissed the depth and

What If...I Love You

complexity of what it's like to be neurodivergent. Knox never needed to understand it, make sense of it, in order to empathize. He always just believed me and accepted me as I am.

I'm in my room unpacking when Knox walks in, staring at his phone, brows pressed together, jaw tight. All the relaxed joy I felt the past few hours quickly sweep away because I know that reality is about to dump a bucket of ice water on us both. "What's wrong?"

"More photos," he sighs, turning his phone to me. It's an image of us from this morning. Facing each other at the campsite just after all the campers drove away. We're standing so close, we could share breath. Knox is looking down at me with heat in his eyes; I'm looking up at him like I'm hypnotized by this golden, beautiful man, and honestly, at that moment, I was. We're not touching, but the angle of this photo makes it look like an intimate moment when in fact, Knox was just asking me if I was ready to leave. In the next photo, he's picking a twig out of my hair, but in the photo, it looks like he's gently caressing me.

I hand the phone back to him and swallow around the lump in my throat. Damn, those photos were hot, even though in reality we were just coming down from the emotional high of the night before. We're just two friends who are trying to reconcile and deal with our baggage.

I think.

"I can't believe they followed us," he says. "This is getting ridiculous. I'm going to find out who is taking these photos and put a stop to this now. They're trying to create a narrative that is just not true."

Hearing him say that should make me feel better, but I can't deny the confusing mix of disappointment and a longing that bubbles up inside of me.

"I think I should meet with Autistics United," I say.

"Maybe if I explain to them the purpose of the Calm Monitor, they'll understand that it's not the problem and focus on getting Caldwell to change its practices."

"No, Renee, I don't think it's a good idea. They'll only use it to advance their agenda. I know what I have to do," he says determinedly. "I'm going to end the contract with Caldwell. If we separate from them completely, then they'll have no choice but to turn their attention to Caldwell and it'll take the heat off you."

Hearing him say that gives me a momentary sense of relief.

"Are you sure?" I ask, looking closely at him. I know how much it means to him to be able to succeed in his new role. To protect his father's legacy. Breaking a multimillion-dollar contract will come with a lot of backlash from his board and shareholders.

He grabs my hands and looks down at me, his cinnamon eyes shining with determination and conviction. "Yes, I'm sure. It's the right thing to do. This is not the way I want to state my tenure as CEO. We will not work with Caldwell and we will not put you in a position to see your designs used in an unethical way. I'll talk to the board tomorrow and let them know."

I wrap my arms around his waist and press my face to his chest. "Thank you, Knox."

He holds me close, his chest rising and falling evenly, and suddenly I can breathe again too. We stay that way a while, just breathing together. My body relaxes and all the stress and anxiety begin to fall away. But eventually, I force myself to pull away. "I'm so tired. I think I'm going to call it a day," I say, putting some space between us. He gives me a nod and a soft, knowing smile before heading to the door.

"Wait. Knox?" He turns back to look at me. "Do you want to watch *The Opening*?"

His face lights up in a smile. "Of course, Nay," and so I

spend the evening watching my favorite show with my favorite person.

———

SLEEP HAS NEVER COME easy to me.

Changes in my routine, stress, a strange new environment can all trigger night terrors, insomnia, and racing thoughts. After watching a few episodes of *The Opening* with Knox, it takes me a while to fall asleep. My thoughts ping between my conversation with Knox, the new feelings emerging between us, and what I will do about Renox. Even without the campaign against the Calm Monitor, I've been struggling to keep Renox afloat for more than a year. Knox's decision to cancel the deal with Caldwell will definitely take some of the pressure off, but will it be enough to save the company? Probably not.

Eventually, I fall into a restless sleep only to wake up in a panic, sweating, panting, and standing in the middle of the bedroom. It takes me a moment to realize that I must've had a night terror.

Knox comes running into the room, dressed in only a loose pair of shorts, his bare chest heaving, and comes toward me slowly. "Renee?" he calls softly.

"I'm awake," I assure him. He's more than familiar with my night terrors. When we lived together, it was so much worse. Back then, I didn't understand what triggered them. But a consistent sleep schedule and managing stress have helped to reduce them.

"I'm okay," I say, climbing back into bed. "It's been a while since I had one," I add.

He climbs into bed next to me, not convinced, and looks closely at me.

"I promise I'm okay." But the crack in my voice gives me away. He doesn't say anything else, just gets under the covers and pulls me into his arms and my heart rate begins to slow, my muscles unfurl, and then finally I find rest.

I wake up the next morning swaddled in strong arms, my back pressed to Knox's chest. I don't know that we've ever been so physically close. We always hugged. He was one of the few people I could stand to be touched by. In fact, I often sought the comfort of his touch.

He gets up and I instantly miss his touch, his hands on me, but before I can fully grieve the loss, he's back with a cool, damp washcloth to wipe my tear-streaked face and neck. I don't even remember crying. He brushes my hair back from my face. In all my stressing before bed, I hadn't tied my curls up. He grabbed the satin scarf from my bedside and started wrapping my hair for me. It made me remember the ways he used to take care of me when I was too tired to move, the comfort that I felt knowing he was one of the few people who understood what I needed. How gentle and tender he could be.

But now it's morning and I can't help but replay the night's events and think about how good it feels to be in his arms. I've never been good at sharing a bed with anyone. The few relationships were short lived. Very few men have patience for the quirks of an autistic girlfriend. I never allowed my partners to sleep over. If they did, I insisted they sleep in another room. I just wouldn't be able to sleep with someone next to me. The sound of their breathing or, even worse, snoring. The shifting of a body next to me on the bed. Everything that might be comforting for someone else made sleep impossible for me. Yet, somehow, I managed to sleep soundly right next to Knox. It's like our bodies synced together and, in the process, we found peace in each other. Or maybe it was just the emotional exhaustion after such a busy few days.

I start to squirm, preparing to move out of his embrace in the hopes that I'll be able to think clearly without him so close to me.

"It's too early for your brain to be working this hard. Just relax." His sleep-thick voice rumbles through me. The vibration sends tingles down the back of my neck to the base of my spine.

"Mmm … I should … probably get up?" I don't mean for it to come out as a question, but right now my brain and my body seem to be having a disagreement and there's no one to mediate the conflict.

Knox slings his leg over mine and tightens his arms around me. "Not yet. I need a little more Nay time."

"Okay," I say, letting my body win this round. I relax into him a little more. But in the process, I press my ass back into him and he lets out a sharp gasp and stiffens slightly. I feel his stiffness grow more pronounced against my ass, but I don't move and neither does he. His hands start to roam, slowly, exploring, testing. I can tell he's watching me. Watching how I react to his touch.

This slow-moving wave of warmth builds from my face down my chest, settling right between my thighs. His fingers trail a line down my bare arms, leaving goose bumps in their wake.

My nipples pebble beneath my thin tank, turning into sharp points. His hands move down to my stomach and under my shirt, and I let out a soft sigh. I realize that I've been moving my hips, pressing into him with each breath. His hand moves under my shirt to massage my breasts. He grabs one firmly in his hands, pressing down on my nipple, and it's exactly the right pressure and firmness. I have no idea how he knows what I need, but he does. I let out a garbled sound as he massages my breasts and begin to roll my hips onto him. The warmth between my thighs has turned molten.

I feel my own wetness and squeeze my thighs together, never losing contact with his thick hardness, now practically nuzzled between my ass cheeks.

Knox watches me with curiosity and fire in his eyes. "Tell me what you want, Nay."

I can't find words. I don't know what to say. I wouldn't even know where to begin.

He leans his face into my shoulder. "Tell me."

The pressure on my breast increases and I yell, "Yes!"

"Okay, now we're getting somewhere." His touch becomes even firmer, almost bruising, and it's exactly what I need. I'm so close to losing all control.

"Ah, I remember now," he says. "You need pressure. You used to like it when I gave you tight hugs. It helped to calm you. I wonder if…" His voice trails off, but his hands finish the sentence. He drags his hands down to my pussy, slipping them beneath my panties and firmly grabbing hold. I buck off the bed into his hands and he meets my thrust, pressing his palm onto my clit as his middle finger dips inside my channel.

I flop down onto my back, giving him better access, and I see the hunger in his eyes. It almost takes me over the edge.

"Oh, my beautiful Nay. I want to make you come so fucking hard, you're screaming my name. Is that okay, baby?" I nod frantically, unable to look away. "I could spend days, months, years learning all the mysteries of your body."

He pulls up my shirt with his free hand and begins sucking on my nipples. A deep moan escapes my throat, and if I wasn't a mess of pleasure, I might actually be embarrassed by how desperate I feel to take everything he's giving me. His hand continues to work me between my thighs, pressing hard on my clit while fucking me with one, then two fingers. I grab hold of his head as he sucks on my breasts and then he bites down, hard, and I explode, screaming my orgasm and crying his name over and over as waves and waves of pleasure roll through me.

He lets me ride it out. Licks and blows softly on my breasts while the rhythm of his hand becomes softer and more soothing until I'm purring like a kitten. He finally removes his hand, brings it to his mouth, and licks his fingers clean, his eyes closed like he's savoring his favorite meal. I can't take my eyes off him. I'm mesmerized, like he's a magician who's just pulled off the most incredible magic trick, and maybe he is because no one has ever made me come like that before.

Finally, he turns to me with a softness in his eyes that's both familiar and somehow new. There's something more there that I've never seen before, or maybe I just didn't notice. He plants kisses all over my face and down my chest, kissing both my inner thighs before planting one last soft, lingering kiss right on my pussy while looking deep into my eyes before he gets up. His cock is fighting against his boxer briefs, but he doesn't seem at all bothered by his unfulfilled state. He steps out of his briefs, giving me a full view of what he's working with, and my mouth starts to water at the sight.

He smirks at me before walking toward the bathroom and shutting the door. I hear the shower turn on and I can already picture him in there, using his hand to seek his own release. I know he's daring me to follow him in, but I'm just not that brave. So instead, I jump out of bed, pull on some shorts and a hoodie, and head toward the kitchen to make coffee, hoping that caffeine and a little distance will help me to make sense of what just happened between us.

Chapter 13

RENEE

MAYBE I'M RUNNING AWAY, or maybe I just need to see my best friend. Either way, I text Jordyn and ask her to meet up for coffee.

I need some space from Knox to make sense of what just happened between us. When Knox came out of my bathroom, showered, with a towel wrapped around his hips, he didn't say anything about what happened between us. I don't know that I would have been able to talk about it just yet. We've known each other for seven years. He was my best friend, my business partner, my closest confidant for the first three years and a ghost lingering in the back of my mind for the four years we didn't speak. Never once did I imagine that we were capable of such sexual heat. No one has ever made me feel the way he did in one morning.

I've had two serious boyfriends who were my only sexual partners in my life. Sex always felt like a chore, like something that was expected of me, and I played the role well. But I've never felt completely safe enough to fall apart the way I did when Knox touched me. It was like he overwhelmed all my senses—the way he paid attention and was so patient.

Sometimes I find it hard to climax with a partner, and eventually they get impatient and I just fake it or tell them it's okay and that I don't need to come. But instead of seeing my body as some kind of broken machine that it was his responsibility to fix, he seemed almost awed by me. Like he loved the idea of getting to figure out what would turn me on and make me come apart.

So of course I got the hell out of there as quickly as possible.

When I told him I was going to see Jordyn, he offered to tag along so it could be the three of us again like old times, but I told him I need to talk to her alone. He gave me a knowing look and a kiss on the head and walked me to the door. "I'll see you later, Nay," he called over his shoulder as he walked away.

"Um, okay."

"Oh, it's going to be so much better than okay. Just you wait." I hear him laugh and I roll my eyes.

I love this time of year. The scorching summer temps give way to a cool seventy degrees in October. The sun is shining outside and I watch people walk by the café window in their light fall attire, enjoying the perfect weather on a chill Sunday afternoon. I sip my chai latte and wait for Jordyn to join me at the spot we've made our gathering place since college. It's a wonder this very cool boho coffee house has survived so long. Somehow the Brew House has managed to survive being swept away by the bigger coffee chains, and I'm grateful that there is still one constant in my life even as we've watched everything else we love about this city evolve and change over the last decade.

When we were college students, it was obvious to us that Austin was on its way to becoming the Southwest capital of tech, which is why we stayed and founded Renox Tech here instead of going to Silicon Valley. Sometimes I wonder if the real reason I stayed was because of Knox. Would I have moved back to California if he weren't here?

Jordyn comes into the coffee shop loaded down with bags. She's got a yoga mat under one arm, a gym bag, and her work purse in the other.

"What's all this stuff? It's Sunday. Take a load off." I dryly chuckle at my own joke and Jordyn just snorts and shakes her head.

"Good morning. I just came from yoga class and now I'm planning to camp out here for the rest of the afternoon and finish writing some learning plans for my students. I forgot how much work being an educator is, but it does feel good to be back working with students, teachers, and parents." I can tell from the light in Jordyn's eyes that she is happy in her new job as a learning specialist. She's doing what she loves and I'm so proud of her.

"So what was so urgent that you called an impromptu coffee meet? Is everything okay over at Knox's place? Is he being a dickhead? Because I will get him back in line. Just say the word."

I huff and try to respond, but my mouth just keeps falling open and closed like a dying fish. Jordyn frowns and begins to look concerned.

"What happened?" she asks seriously.

"We had … a moment, I guess?"

She looks puzzled and studies my face before some kind of understanding begins to form in her expression. She quickly looks around and then leans in across the table with a slow smile forming on her lips. "Finally!"

I jerk back. "What do you mean, finally?"

"I mean that my two best friends have been in love with each other since college and it sounds like you've finally gotten out of your own way and done something about it … unless I'm reading this all wrong?"

I scrub a hand over my face, trying to figure out how this conversation has only managed to make me even more confused.

"Jordyn, Knox and I have never felt like that for each other. Our relationship has always been platonic. Which is why our little encounter this morning doesn't make any sense. It's the last thing we need right now if we're going to work out a solution to the Caldwell problem and maybe fix our friendship. Sex will only complicate things more."

Jordyn just sits back and looks at me, a frown creasing her brow. "Tell me something. How does he make you feel?"

I'm caught off guard by her question. But I think about it. "He's always made me feel safe. He … understands me in ways no one else does. This morning was earth shattering … but I just don't—"

"Let me stop you right there. Honey, do you know how many times I've been able to say the words 'safe', 'understood', and 'earth shattering' in the same breath?" She doesn't even wait for me to respond. "Never. Knox is your person and you are his. I've always known. I think he has for a long time but didn't want to scare you away. But I can't sit back and let you ignore what is right in front of you, Renee. Knox loves you. He always has, and I know that you love him."

"How do you know that?"

"Because even after he hurt you by walking away from the company, you never stopped having feelings for him. You're so hurt because you knew that you were missing him. You could have changed the name of the company and erased all hints of him in your life, but you didn't. Tell me you see that."

I sit quietly for a moment and stare out of the shop

window, replaying moments from my relationship with Knox. One moment snags on my mind more than others: the expression on his face when I told him I was moving out. There was something so wrong about that moment that I just couldn't quite figure out. And then the other night, he said I left him first. But why would he think that when we worked together every day? I only moved out so that he'd have more space, more freedom to live his life, maybe move in with his girlfriend without my burdening him. But maybe I got it wrong.

"But..." Jordyn adds hesitantly.

"But what?" I demand.

"Sometimes you give up way too much of yourself when you're with him. It's like you just meld into Knox and stop making your own choices. You're way too comfortable letting him take the lead. I kinda think it was a good thing that you moved out and got to step out on your own professionally. You're so much more..."

"More what?"

"Just more, now. I don't want you to lose yourself in him again." She leans forward on the table. "Girl, you are the sun. Don't let that man steal your shine."

I sit back for a moment, warmed through with gratitude for my friend. I smile at her. "Don't think I didn't catch that *Grey's Anatomy* reference." I laugh.

"You like how I sneaked that in?" We both giggle, remembering the hours she forced me to watch the series with her in her dorm room. I take a deep breath; she's right. The old me would have sat back, content to let Knox take the lead—waited for him to decide to start the conversation, decide the future of our relationship. But I've been standing on my own for a long time. I may not be one-hundred-percent sure of what I want right now, but I don't want to shy away from starting the conversation.

"Jordyn, I gotta go." I jump up and grab my things.

Jordyn doesn't at all seem surprised. She just nods with a knowing smirk on her face. She pulls a stack of papers out of her work bag and drops them on the table. "Uh-huh. Tell Knox he owes me dinner. In fact, you both do."

Chapter 14

KNOX

AFTER RENEE LEFT to go have coffee with Jordyn, I dove into some work to keep my mind off what happened between us this morning. I would be lying if I said I've never thought about what her body would feel like under mine. I've thought about it a lot over the years. It was especially difficult when I was close to her as a friend without any chance of us having sex.

I used to focus a lot on just making sure that she was okay. My touch was always meant to comfort, so in those moments when she was most vulnerable, I never wanted to betray her trust by trying to fuck her.

But this morning was different.

We've never shared a bed before. It felt so good to have her back in my arms again. I pressed close to her and held her tight like she might disappear.

I never meant for it to turn sexual, but then she pushed her soft, round ass right into my dick. I thought she would pull away when she felt me harden but she didn't.

I try to focus on work, but my thoughts keep turning back to Renee, wondering how she feels about what happened between us. There is some part of me that feels anxious about the possibility of her deciding she doesn't want this, doesn't want me. I don't know if I can handle that, not after what happened between us. But I knew that she wasn't ready to talk about it this morning. She could barely look at me, and I could see the wheels in her head turning, trying to decide how she felt about it. But there was no mistaking what her body wanted as I made her unravel. Watching her fall apart under my touch blew my mind.

She's never looked more beautiful than when she was orgasming just from my fingers. I can't wait to be inside her and watch her lose it while I fill her up.

"Fuck!" I slam my laptop closed, too distracted to work. As I head back to the kitchen for more coffee, I check the clock. Renee's been out for more than an hour. We need to talk as soon as she gets back. I need to come clean and just tell her how I feel about her, about us. Maybe it's too soon to ask her for more than friendship, but I at least need to know it's an option.

I hear the elevator doors quietly open and close and my heart lurches in my chest. I set the coffee mug down and head back out into the foyer to greet her. When I see her face, I can tell that she has something big to say.

"Hey, how's Jordyn?"

"Good. Busy with her new job. But she loves it."

She takes off her shoes and drops her bag by the door. Seeing her things around my place makes me feel all kinds of possessive and attached, like I never want her to leave. Never want to live anywhere she isn't, ever again.

I wait, wanting her to speak first. I can tell she's searching for the words. She walks toward me, finally meeting my eyes, and there's so much there. So much I can't quite read over my own feelings, desires, and desperate wants. I just wait and remember to breathe.

"I need to ... ask you about something," she says hesitantly.

"Ask me anything you want."

She continues walking into the living room and I follow her. She sits on the couch and looks out the window for a moment before turning back toward me.

"Uh ... remember when we lived together right after college?"

I'm not sure I like where this is going, but I stay in it. I can't quite bring myself to sit until I know where this conversation is going, so I stand in front of her awkwardly on the other side of the coffee table, like I'm a contestant in a game show and she's one of the celebrity hosts.

"Yeah, of course. How could I ever forget the tiny two-bedroom with the paper-thin walls? We spent a lot of evenings listening to our neighbors through the walls, making up stories about what they were doing." I'm babbling and I do not know why.

"Yeah, that place was so weird. The reason I asked is that Jordyn said some things to me today that made me rethink that time. Maybe there were some things I missed..."

Suddenly I get it. Renee has this uncanny ability to miss details of things in the moment but remember them with shocking clarity years later. It's like her brain stores all the information but just takes longer to process it. Eventually, she does, and her insight is sharp as hell. I finally sit down with her on the couch.

"What do you mean? Tell me what you remember."

"I remember that we were really close, and I loved living with you."

"I loved living with you, too," I say, taking her hand in mine.

"But ... I also felt like I was holding you back. You kept having these short-lived relationships that would only last a few months, and then you met Val and the two of you seemed so perfect together ... I felt like I was in the way. Maybe all the time you spent taking care of me—your tired, anxious autistic friend and business partner—was making it difficult for you to make your relationships work. So I moved out to give you space to have your own life. Our lives were already so tangled with Renox; living together was just too much."

I stare at Renee in shock. Her moving out set off a chain of events that led to us being apart for the last four years. She watches me for a moment before she continues.

"I just wanted you to be happy. But the day I told you I was moving out, the look on your face—"

"I was devastated."

"Why? I don't understand."

"Renee, I've been in love with you for as long as I can remember. When you told me you were leaving, it was like you kicked me in the chest. It felt like you didn't want me."

"I don't understand. You had girlfriends."

"You had boyfriends. Did you ever notice that the only time I was dating was when you were dating someone? It was the only way to keep myself distracted from how jealous I was that someone else got to touch you."

We both sit quietly, staring off in different directions as the pieces of our history begin to click back together.

"You broke my heart when you left. And ... I think that when I quit and went to work with my dad, maybe for a moment I was a little relieved that I didn't have to see you every day anymore. I know that's a fucked-up thing to say…"

Renee jumps up off the couch, and when I see her face, I know I've said the wrong thing.

"So you left to punish me for something I didn't even know I'd done. That's so fucked up, Knox."

"It wasn't like that. I wasn't trying to punish you. I just … I don't know what I was doing." I drop my head into my hands. Nothing I'm saying is coming out right. I'm probably fucking up any chance I have with her. But I can't give up.

Renee paces back and forth, her eyes on the small track of floor she travels beneath her. She's biting her lip and clenching her hands, all the signs that she's getting overwhelmed. Shit, I'm getting overwhelmed and I don't have a nervous system on a constant hair trigger.

"Renee, please come here. Sit with me."

She stops and looks at the spot I pat on the couch before heaving a heavy sigh and sitting down. She sits and we instantly fold into the position that always gives her comfort. She slides into the space between my legs and forms her petite body into a ball, and I fold in around her with my arms and legs. I lean back on the arm of the couch and wait as I feel her slowly relax deeper into my chest. When our breathing begins to sync, I speak again. "It was always you I wanted. I never wanted anyone else. I would rather be right here with you on your hardest days than be with anyone else. That has always been true." We're both quiet for a moment as my words sink in.

"I'm so sorry that I left. That I hurt you," she says. "I wish you had told me how you really felt."

I kiss the top of her head, breathing in her sweetly scented curls.

"I know. I'm sorry. I was afraid to lose you. I wanted to be your safe place. I never wanted you to think that I was one of those guys who would use your vulnerability to get in your pants. I was your friend and that will always be enough for me. If you tell me you don't want this, don't want to be with me, I'll accept that. As long as I get to have you in my life."

We're quiet for a long spell. Just breathing together. Just close and connected.

She sighs, leaning her head into my chest. "I gave up on the possibility of ever finding someone who would want to be with me. Relationships have always been so hard. Sex has never felt right or natural. But this morning was unlike anything I've ever experienced." Renee pulls out of my hold and I instantly miss the connection, but then she shocks the shit out of me by turning around and straddling me. My hands quickly go to her hips and I start to harden when I see the desire in her eyes.

"I want you, Knox. I've never let myself even consider the possibility that we could be more than friends, and that's all my stuff, I know. But you've always been the standard that I've measured every other man against. Every relationship has fallen short of what I feel when I'm with you. I feel safe, but I also feel … this … I can't explain it. I just want to touch you. I want to feel your hands on me."

My hands start to move as she speaks. Watching her get flustered and heated, trying to find the words to describe how she feels for me, only turns me on more. My mouth goes to her neck. I graze my teeth along her flesh. I pull back to look at her again. Eyes glassy, jaw slack, full lips parted. Her soft, delicate hands roam my chest.

"I get it, Nay. You wanna fuck me," I say, smirking.

She looks shocked and then begins to laugh. "Oh, my God. I can't believe we're doing this. I've never … no, that's not true. I have thought about it."

My eyebrows shoot up. "Oh, yeah? Tell me what you've thought about."

She gets shy, sucking her bottom lip between her teeth, and I get even harder. Shy, bashful Renee is now my favorite look. "Tell me," I say gripping her hips and grinding up into her.

She sucks in a breath at the feel of my dick pressing against her pussy. I can feel the heat between her thighs even through a layer of pants and can only imagine how wet she must be getting. And we haven't even gotten started yet.

"I used to touch myself and imagine you sitting across from me on the couch, working your dick with your hand. Oddly, I could never conjure up a fantasy where you were actually touching me, but I spent a lot of time imagining you jerking off while I watched." She covers her face with her hands, looking thoroughly embarrassed. "Is that weird?" she says while hiding her face.

I pull her hands away, kissing each palm and then pressing them between us so she can feel my hard-on.

"No, baby, that's not weird at all. You can watch me whenever you want. You want to know what I fantasize about?" She looks into my eyes, curiosity mixed with desire pouring out of her beautiful brown irises. "I've had lots of fantasies about you, but my favorite involves you naked and riding my dick while sitting on my lap. I have my hand wrapped around your neck and my other massaging your clit, and you just fall apart screaming my name while I whisper praise into your ear." As I describe this scene, her breathing gets even heavier and her eyelids droop.

I pull her face to mine and kiss her deeply. Renee has a vivid imagination, so I know that my words are just the right kind of foreplay for us, but I'm not ready to stop at telling her what I want to do to her.

"How does that sound to you? Would you like me to fuck you like that, my sweet Nay?

"Yes," she breathes. The word is barely out of her mouth before I'm lifting us both off the couch and striding toward the bedroom with her still wrapped around my waist. I get her into the bedroom and waste no time stripping her clothes off.

"I can't wait to be inside you. I've wanted this for so fucking long. But first, I need to taste that sweet pussy of yours. This morning just wasn't enough. I need to dip my tongue right into you. Is that okay, baby? Can I make you cum in my mouth?"

Renee pauses and I can immediately tell that she's left her body and gone into her head. I stop short of pulling off her pants and kneel before her with my hands resting on her thighs. "Tell me what's on your mind. First thought."

She sighs, dropping back on the bed to stare at the ceiling before admitting, "I'm thinking that no one has ever made me come like that. In fact, I can count on one hand the number of times I've come during sex. This morning was the third."

The thought of Renee having sex with anyone else pisses me off, but the thought of her being left unsatisfied makes me fucking murderous. Like I want to track down every asshole who ever touched her and make them pay for not treating her the way she deserves. But I put those murderous thoughts aside because there's no way she's going to ever feel like that with me.

I slowly climb up her body, kissing and caressing her softly as I do. "Renee…" I wait for her to meet my eyes. "No one knows your body the way I do. Do you remember what I said this morning? I want to know all the mysteries of your body. I want to play and explore with you because I love you. Do you trust me?" She nods without hesitation. "Do you feel safe with me?"

"Yes," she says.

I slide her panties off and toss them aside, leaving her fully naked on my bed.

"Then trust me when I tell you, you will come for me. Together we're going to discover all the ways you like to be fucked, and I'm going to give it to you, give you everything you need, until you're begging for more." Then I drop back down to my knees so I'm in line with her sweet spot. "Nay, baby, touch yourself for me. Show me how you get off. Show me what you like."

She reaches a hand down to her pussy and begins to rub in a steady circle around her outer lips, keeping her very sensitive clit protected but pressing hard at a steady pace.

She dips her fingers down below to gather some wetness and then continues to rub. My mouth waters at the sight, and I stare in awe at her working herself up. I move closer, kissing her inner thighs and breathing in the smell of her arousal. I'm so hard I have to strip out of my sweats and grab hold of my shaft as I watch her.

I can tell that she's close, but I want to move from lesson to practice, so I push her hands away and replace them with my own, using the same circling movement and pace as she did. "Like this? Is this how you like it?" She nods frantically. "If you need more pressure, just press my hands down more to let me know, okay?"

Her slick hand falls over my mine and she presses down more. I continue to rub her pussy with one hand while stroking myself with the other and she lets out a soft moan. I only remove my hands from my dick to grab her hips, pull her just to the edge of the bed, and press my mouth to her pussy, using my tongue to give her the same movement and pressure as my hand.

She bucks up off the bed and cries out, and that's when I know I've got her close to the edge. She begins to chant a steady, needy "ah … ah" that goes straight to my balls. She grabs my head, pressing it down, and begins fucking my face. I can't help but smile into her pussy. She could suffocate me right here and I'd die a happy man. As she gets closer to her climax, her movements pick up pace.

"Oh, oh, oh, Knox. Yes, yes, just like that. Omigod. I can't believe this feels so good." In the next second, she's coming hard, her juices running down my chin. I slowly lap up her sweet nectar, not wanting to waste a drop. She goes completely limp, and I slide up her body, licking my lips as I trail kisses up her torso and suck each nipple into my mouth, releasing it with a pop. Every time I make her fall apart, it feels like I've won a prize.

She watches me as I slowly travel up her body, a soft, satisfied glow on her face unlike anything I've ever seen. I've seen her focused, bubbling with ideas, anxious, inquisitive, afraid, confused, exhausted, but I've never seen her well-fucked orgasm face, and I have to say this might be my favorite look on her. I hold myself up on my arms so I can look down at her and take in her face.

"We're not done yet, baby," I say as I caress her cheek, brushing a soft curl off her face. "I'm not done making you mine. I won't be done until I'm buried deep inside you. Are you ready for that?"

"Yes, I want to feel you," she says in a sexy, breathy way I've never heard from her before.

"Let me grab a condom."

I go to move off her, but she grabs my arm, holding me in place. "It's okay. I've been on the pill forever. I don't want to use a condom if that's okay with you."

A slow smile spreads on my face. "That's more than okay," I say, as I spread her legs and line myself up at the meeting of her thighs. I look at her once more, knowing everything between us is about to change forever. "I love you, Nay," I say, as I slowly push inside her. I watch her face for discomfort or even a hint of uncertainty. But all I see is this blossoming of pleasure, euphoria.

I feel it too. The way our bodies feel together. Slowly, I slide inside her until our hips are pressed together and I just stay there. Close my eyes and just feel it. Feel what it is to finally be home.

Renee grabs my face and kisses me. "Knox, fuck me. Now," she whispers into my mouth, and so I do. I begin a slow, rhythmic pace, my hips circling and pressing deep into her. Her head falls back, her eyes shut, as she meets each of my thrusts. I don't know why I'm surprised that we're so sexually compatible, but it's so much better than I ever dreamed it would be. I grab her legs, bending them and pressing them beneath my shoulders so I can get deeper, and I fuck her harder. She looks at me like I just opened a portal to another dimension. Overwhelmed in the best possible way.

"What are you doing to me?" she sputters around the pace of my thrust.

"I'm giving you everything you deserve and so much more."

I pull out, pull her off the bed. I sit on the edge and then sit her on my dick with her back pressed to my chest. I fuck up into her, holding tightly onto her hips, and then slide one hand around her neck and the other down to her clit.

My instincts tell me that what Renee needs is to be overwhelmed with so much sensation, she can't get stuck in her head and think her way out of her own pleasure. So I press firmly against her throat and her clit, and then, when she least expects it, I bite her shoulder. She completely falls apart as a second orgasm slams into her tight little body. I feel her clenching and pulsing around me as she comes. I stand her up and bend her forward, move my hand from her throat to her hair and continue to fuck into her at a frantic pace. I turn her toward the bed, bend her over it with her shoulders pressed to the bed, and slap her ass hard. She moans. Well, shit, I'm learning a lot about what my baby likes right now. I slap her ass three times in succession and her pussy strangles my dick. I rub the red cheek to relieve the sting.

"Oh, Nay, you take my dick so well. I can't believe it took us so long to get here. Now that I've had you, I'm never giving you up. You're mine, baby. Say it."

"I'm yours," she moans. I lie on top of her, pressing her to the bed in our favorite position, my front to her back, and I can't hold it off anymore. I wish I could stay buried inside her forever, but my own climax builds and explodes out of me with a sharp groan buried into her hair. I roll off her and pull her close to me. She looks up at me in a soft sleep haze. I think I see love there, but I can't be sure.

She presses her hand to my chest right over my heart and says, "Mine."

"Always." I reply.

Yes, that is love I see. She doesn't even have to say the word. We've always had a language all our own.

Chapter 15

KNOX

I WALK into my office at LyonTech on Monday morning feeling lighter than I have in months. Not since my dad's death, in fact. I can't help but smile, thinking about my night with Renee. What finally happened between us was a long time coming. I won't deny that I thought about it a few dozen thousand times, but the reality was so much better.

I'm just settling in at my desk, checking emails, when Jeffrey walks into my office. "Oh, good, I was just about to ping you to schedule a meeting." I chuckle nervously.

Jeffrey is not going to be happy with what I'm about to tell him. The board won't be happy about it either, but it's the best decision. We need to cancel the deal with Caldwell. It doesn't look good for us to be in business with a company known for its unethical treatment of its patients, and it definitely isn't something that Renee would ever want her work associated with. It will mean losing a major contract, one that's worth eighty million dollars, but it will also instantly take the target off our back, and instead maybe even start a conversation about the ethics of tech design. That's something I could definitely put my name behind. The profit we lose we can make up, but the reputational hit would be much harder to recover from. At least, that's the way I intend to pitch it to Jeffrey and the board.

"Yes, I agree. We need to decide next steps for how we're going to close this deal with Caldwell and minimize the blowback. Were you and Ms. Johnson able to negotiate or compromise?"

"We both agree that the best course of action is to cancel the deal with Caldwell."

Jeffrey's eyes widen, and his jaw clamps shut in a hard line. He drops into the chair in front of my desk, suddenly looking very tired, and sighs. "Knox, you can't make a decision like this based on emotion."

Now it's my turn to look shocked. But he continues. "If the photos that have surfaced recently are any indication, it's clear to me and everyone else that you have very strong feelings for this woman. But this is business. This is not how your father would handle things."

I take a deep breath and unclench my jaw. When I feel capable of speaking again, I look at him. "Jeffrey, I will not start my tenure as CEO of this company by closing a deal with a company that could potentially hurt our credibility. This isn't about my relationship with Renee. My name is on the building and that means something to me. I'm doing what's best for my company," I tell him. But it feels like I'm speaking to a brick wall.

"There's no way you'll get the board to agree to this." He shakes his head. "You think Caldwell is the first company we've sold products to that has a questionable track record? We contract with the U.S. Special Forces, for Christ's sake!" he says, tossing his hands in the air.

He does have a point there, but I'm undeterred. This is the

right thing to do. But I do need to make a stronger case to the board to get them to vote in my favor. And I can't get a deal this large canceled without their approval.

"I'll handle it," I press, but I'm not feeling as confident as I was when I walked into the office this morning. The board is going to be an issue here. If Jeffrey is pushing back, then Michael will be a brick wall.

"Jeffrey, I need you to know that I want what is best for this company. We have a chance to reframe the conversation and be at the forefront of ethical tech. I want that to be my legacy as CEO."

He looks at me closely for a moment before his expression shifts into something almost more agreeable. "You're just like him, you know." Shaking his head, he stands. "Stubborn." He turns and heads toward my office door but stops and turns back to me. "If you have any shot of pulling this off, you're going to need to get the majority of the board to vote in your favor. I would start with Klein and Markston. If you can get them on board, then Michael might be swayed as well."

I nod, appreciating actionable advice. It feels like the first time he's offered even an inch of support for my ideas, so I'll take it. "Thanks, Jeffrey."

I try to return to my work, but long after Jeffrey has left, I feel this growing dread, knowing that my first major act as CEO could cost the company millions. *You're not going to make yourself any allies this way, son.* "I know, Dad," I say, looking at his photo on my desk. As much as I want to live up to his legacy, I also know I've got to find a way to carve out my own.

Chapter 16

RENEE

I WALK BACK into the Renox Tech offices after being away for over a week and an undercurrent of anxiety washes over me as I consider what awaits me. The week I was off was the first week I had taken off in more than two years. It was only when I was away from the office that it really hit me just how stressful it has been to run this business. I love being a designer, but Renox Tech requires so much more from me.

When Knox and I started this company, we had an understanding that he would run the business side and I would be the project lead. When he left, I was forced to take over running the business. It wasn't like our start-up could afford to hire someone to do business management, so it fell to me. As much as I love Renox, I miss being able to focus on the part of the work that I enjoy the most: designing. More often than not, I end up working solo because I have to split my limited attention and energy between business management and my own design work.

My team is busy at work—collaborating, brainstorming, talking through ideas together. When I walk in, everyone looks up from the whiteboard they're standing around, surprised to see me.

I wave to them. "I'm back."

"Welcome back," Davis says. The rest of the group nods and smiles. It feels so different in here now that Jordyn is no longer working.

Sasha, the new office manager who is taking over for Jordyn, gets up and follows me into my office. She spent a month being trained by Jordyn before she left and has already proven that she's more than capable of keeping things running while I was out of the office. The few times I did check in over the last week, she gave me updates and anticipated any questions I might have about project timelines.

"Hey, Sasha. How's it goin'?"

"Good. All projects are on schedule. The team has been doing really great work, but there have been some questions from the team about what's going on with the Calm Monitor and how it might impact our work. I think it might help if you gave us an update."

I knew this was coming. I honestly just have no idea what to tell them right now. Knox has asked me to trust him to resolve this. He promised to cancel the deal with Caldwell, but do I tell the team that the deal is off before it's even been confirmed to put them all at ease? What if canceling the deal is not enough? What if there are other issues with the Calm Monitor that I'm missing?

"I'm working with LyonTech to address these issues right now, but nothing has been confirmed yet," I say.

She swallows and nods nervously. "And the pictures?"

Those damn pictures. Of course, they've seen them. "The pictures are a lie. There's nothing going on between me and Knox," I say, but as soon as the words are out of my mouth, I realize that's no longer true. "You all know he was my former business partner. Some tabloid journalist is trying to make it look like there's something salacious going on and it's just not true."

"Of course," she quickly responds. "We all trust you and know how much you care about the work. No one here thinks that you would ever put the company or your own reputation at risk … for a man." She rolls her eyes at the very implication. But as she says it, I wonder if that's exactly what I'm doing.

I've gotten two more emails from Autistics United, the group leading this online campaign against the Calm Monitor, asking me to meet with them. Knox has asked me not to take the meeting. To trust him to take care of it. Jordyn's advice from yesterday comes back to me. Am I doing what I've always done with Knox? Am I becoming too passive, too willing to let him take the lead? No, this is nothing like before. We were kids then. I just need time to think this through. But what if … I make the wrong choice and I end up taking my team down with me?

"Sasha, do you mind giving an update to the team? As soon as I have something more concrete to share, I'll get everyone together to talk through the strategy for how we're going to address this."

Sasha's face drops a little before she schools her expression and nods. "Of course, whatever you need." And then she's out the door. I know I should be the one to talk to them, but the thought of facing them right now fills me with panic. I don't think I can answer their questions without admitting that I'm probably not being the leader they need me to be right now. I'm trying not to fall back into old patterns with Knox, and this time, there is so much more at stake than our friendship.

Chapter 17

RENEE

THE MORNING GOES by in a blur. I'm deep in work mode, catching up on emails, reviewing project updates, and sending feedback to my team on their work, when Sasha pops her head into my office to remind me that I have a lunch meeting that I need to leave for in twenty minutes. I check my calendar and see that it's a meeting with a potential new client: the superintendent of a local school district whom we've been trying to pitch so we can redesign their online learning system. This would be our biggest contract to date. Getting them to accept our bid would solve all our money problems and set Renox up to be a real competitor in the education tech market nationally. I quickly review my pitch again and make sure the slide deck is loaded onto my tablet before I head out the door.

The restaurant is only a few blocks away and the weather is perfect, a sunny sixty-five-degree day, the kind of mild weather you can only get in fall in central Texas.

The restaurant comes into view, and I check the time to see that I still have about fifteen minutes before our meeting. I take a moment to myself outside the restaurant to feel the sun on my skin, and breathe and check in with my body for any signals of anxiety or stress the way that my therapist taught me. *I'm okay. I can do this. Renox needs me to do this.* I don't know what the future holds for this company. But I do know that right now, I have to do whatever it takes to make sure we succeed. I owe it to my team.

I suck in a final deep breath and turn to walk into the restaurant—and bump right into someone. "Oh! So sorry," I hear a voice above me say, but I'm too busy trying to stay on my feet to see who it is.

"It's okay," I say, finally finding my footing. I look up at a somewhat familiar face that I can't quite place.

"Hey, it's you. Nice to see you again, Renee Johnson. Listen, I'm sorry about that dinner date." And there it is. I remember him now. He's the last guy I went on a date with before I swore off dating for good.

"Oh" is the only thing I can manage to say.

"Yeah, it wasn't cool for me to ask you out and then try to pitch you. Not cool at all," he says sheepishly.

"Yeah, really not cool. But it's all good. Hope everything worked out for you." I turn to walk around him, wanting to end this conversation as quickly as possible.

"It did," he continues. "I actually got a job at LyonTech." That stops me in my tracks. "And the best part is, I'm working on one of your designs right now. So in a way, it's like we do get to work together."

I turn back to him in confusion. That can't be right. Knox said they would stop work on the Calm Monitor.

"What do you mean?" I ask, hoping that he's wrong. That this is some explanation for why they're moving forward when Knox told me he would end the contract with Caldwell. "I thought you'd ... finished up work on that," I say, choosing my words carefully.

"We're wrapping up some edits to your design and getting it ready to be distributed to Caldwell. They actually moved the timeline for distribution up, which is why I got hired."

My stomach bottoms out and I can't even form words to respond. I just walk away from him and into the restaurant.

"Oh, uh. Good to see you," he calls after me.

I tried try to focus on the meeting with the Lepton school district superintendent, but the entire time, my attention is split between making this pitch and trying to figure out why Knox would lie to me. I walk back to my office after the meeting in a daze. It's only when I'm sitting at my desk again that it hits me I might have just blown a huge opportunity for Renox and all because I was, once again, too distracted by Knox.

Enough.

There's too much at stake to put all my faith in him again. I open my computer and see a notification for a video mentioning Renox Tech online. I click on the clip. It's Autistics United, standing in front of a group of protesters with signs demanding a stop to the Calm Monitor and Caldwell. I hate that one of my designs has become associated with such a place, called out by a group I sincerely respect. For weeks, I've been passively waiting for Knox to do the right thing. He asked me not to meet with the group. But whom does that serve? Maybe the Knox I used to know, the one who cared about doing what's right, is gone. Maybe that Knox will never come back. But I can't sit around and wait for him to find his conscience while my reputation gets destroyed.

"We're trying to open dialogue here. We want a meeting with Renee Johnson," the dark-haired person in the middle says, looking directly into the camera.

Okay. Then let's meet.

Chapter 18

RENEE

THE AUTISTICS UNITED offices in downtown Austin is a small storefront painted in cooling shades of lavender and blue. A beautiful mural covers one wall, with images of people of every size and race, some in wheelchairs or holding canes, with colorful hair and tattoos, and piercing fierce looks from behind glasses. In bold red letters like a banner above their heads, it reads, *Disabled and Proud*.

I look around the table at the three leaders of Autistics United: Marla, Leto, and Del. For weeks, they've been emailing and messaging me on social media, demanding a meeting. I ignored their requests. Knox thought it would only make things worse. But now I wonder if the real reason I didn't take the meeting was that I was afraid to hear what they had to say.

Marla sits directly across from me. Her purple hair is long in the front and shaved on the sides. She has a sleeve of tattoos up one arm. She bobs her leg up and down while flipping a pen through her fingers with her opposite hand. I can't remember the last time I let myself move so freely in a room full of people. As I watch her, it occurs to me that I don't know any other autistic Black women.

She sent me an agenda ahead of the meeting, letting me know exactly what to expect. It seemed like a small thing, but it reduced my anxiety about being here by half. It gave me a chance to reflect on what I wanted to say. Apparently, it's something they do for all their meetings. Even the ones with product designers they've spent weeks protesting.

Leto sits to my left. Slouching back in his seat, typing away, his focus on his tablet in front of him that he uses to communicate. "Thank you for agreeing to meet with us," offers the augmented voice app. "As you can see, I'm nonspeaking, but that doesn't mean I can't communicate." He looks up from his device at me with inquisitive blue eyes. I swallow nervously and nod. "Yet your Calm Monitor would take away my ability to communicate my own needs to caregivers, teachers, and health-care professionals. People who already believe that because I am nonspeaking, I must also be incapable of thought, communication, and self-awareness. Your device would take away my ability to advocate for myself when I am more than capable of asking for what I need." He pauses for a moment to let the weight of his words set in.

I look around the room, taking in what he's just said. My eyes snag on another boldly printed slogan: *Nothing for Use, Without Us.*

"When I built the Calm Monitor, I was thinking about my mother," I say. "I built the thing that I thought would have helped her take care of me when I was an undiagnosed autistic nine-year-old having meltdowns almost daily. I thought about all the times when I could feel the churning sensations of overwhelm building inside me, but I was unable to communicate to her what was happening to me. The buildup would eventually lead to a meltdown. I was thinking about how I could make taking care of someone like me easier. It never occurred to me that I was taking away the ability of autistics to communicate and express their own needs," I confess to them.

I stare at another slogan directly in front of me above Marla's head.

We Have a Right to Exist.

"You have internalized ableism. We've all been there." I turn to my right to look at Del as they speak. They've been sketching away on their notepad quietly since the meeting began. I wonder if they're the artist who did the mural and slogans on the walls. Hearing the soft lilt of their voice for the first time surprises me. There is a small smile on their full lips and strong jaw. Amusement crosses their brown eyes, but it's not cruel; just familiar.

It's like they all know me better than I know myself right now. Because they've been where I am.

I consider their words for a moment. I spent my whole life trying to not be a problem for other people. Trying to not be a burden. It's only now, sitting in a room with autistic advocates, listening to them describe their experiences with ableism, listening to them talk about the ways that they've been harmed by health-care and education systems that treated them like a problem to solve—it's only now, at twenty-seven years old, that I realize my understanding of myself has been shaped by the same systems. How is it that I've been unable to see this until now?

Marla breaks the silence. "We've all been there."

Leto nods in agreement.

We've yet to begin talking about LyonTech or what they're planning for the Calm Monitor. They're still educating me on the impact of my design.

"Your Calm Monitor might have been designed with good intentions," Marla says, "but the impact is that it's yet another tool that teachers, social workers, and caregivers can use to control us, when what they need are more effective tools to help us live independently and take care of ourselves."

I did focus groups. I did research. I tried to design something that would improve the lives of disabled people. But I was focused on the wrong end user. Even ideas with the best of intentions can cause harm.

"You're right," I say. "It doesn't matter what I was intending to do long before LyonTech got their hands on it. The Calm Monitor was going to be a problem. So how do I fix this?"

"Renee, I'm glad you came to us. We want to help. We'll do whatever we can to make sure this technology doesn't become yet another tool of oppression, but you've got to own your part in this as well. Are you willing to do that?" Marla explains.

I don't have to even think about it. I know what I have to do. Beneath the shame I feel at having made a mistake so big is a much greater resolve to make it right. To be accountable and to finally stand for something more than my own ideas. To be accountable to a community. "Yes, I can do that."

"Good," Del says. They hold up the sketch pad. It's not at all what I was expecting. It's a graphic illustration of the meeting with images of each of us and a flow chart of the conversation that looks like it's telling a story. The final image is me joining the group much like the mural on the wall of this space, but now it's like I've been added to it, and more than anything, I want to really belong with them.

Chapter 19

KNOX

I'M PACING the floor of my office on a dreary, rainy Friday morning, trying to think of a way out of this Caldwell deal. All week, I've been meeting with board members to make my pitch, and each time the answer has been an unequivocal no. Not one of them has been willing to put ethics before profits. I know I shouldn't be surprised—you don't build a billion-dollar company by not making some compromises—but that's not the way I want to do business.

At home, I've avoided the conversation with Renee, not wanting her to worry that I haven't found a way to do what I promised her I would do. How can I tell her that I failed? I take a deep breath and stop my pacing. Settling back into my chair, I prepare to make the phone call that I've been avoiding all week. I need to call my board chair, Michael. He's the only one left. If I can convince him, then he'll get everyone else on board. As I pick up my phone and prepare to dial, my assistant Justin rushes in, looking absolutely shook.

"Knox, you need to turn on the TV."

"Ugh! What now? Another protest outside the building?" I turn to look out my office windows down at the street below, but there's no one there. In fact, the protesters have been pretty quiet the last week. Maybe that's a good sign. Maybe they've moved on to a new target and we can slip this under the radar.

"No, it's ... Renee. She did an interview," Justin says.

I stare at him as if he must be joking. That can't be right. Renee wouldn't do something like that without talking to me first. We've seen each other every night this week. We've eaten dinner together; we've watched TV. We've cuddled on the couch. We haven't done much more than that, but I figured she wanted to take it slow. We've only been back in each other's lives for like two weeks.

Justin turns on the TV as I sit there in stunned silence.

The sunny, bright colors of the *Morning Today* set fill my fifty-inch TV screen. The host, Terry Mills, looks directly into the camera. "Technology influences every part of our life. Most of us barely remember a time before smartphones, smart TV, and smart watches, but with tech companies creating so many of the devices that are essential to our everyday life, we have to consider the ethical implications of how these tech devices impact our quality of life. Especially for those amongst us who are the most vulnerable. Joining me today is product designer and CEO of Renox Tech, Renee Johnson. Thank you for joining us, Renee."

When the camera pans to Renee, I feel like I've been kicked in the gut. I sit there watching the entire interview, dumbfounded. But I can't deny that Renee looks amazing up there. She's poised, confident, and fierce. She's ripping my heart right out of my chest but has never looked more beautiful.

"When I created Calm Monitor, I thought I was helping autistic people like me to have a tool to help communicate when they were in distress. But what I've come to learn from disability activists at Autistics United is that, in fact, what I did was take away their ability to communicate for themselves. Disabled people have a right to advocate for themselves, to communicate what they need, and to have their needs met on their own terms. I didn't understand that before. But I get it now." Then she turns to the camera and I already know what's coming.

"Which is why I am asking LyonTech to do two things. First, end their contract with Caldwell Treatment Facilities immediately. Their treatment facilities have been known for using punitive methods to control and abuse people with neurodevelopment disorders in their care. LyonTech has an obligation to end its relationship with them immediately. Second, do not distribute the Calm Monitor in its current design. I am happy to offer my services pro bono to redesign the monitor so it can be used by disabled people to monitor their own nervous-system regulation and use that information to communicate their needs. I'm assembling a team of disabled designers who have agreed to work on this project with me, and Renox will commit to oversight from this team in all future designs."

Long after the interview ends, I sit in my chair, staring at the now-dark TV. Justin has long since gone back to his desk, getting that I probably needed a moment to get over the shock of watching Renee throw us under the bus. I sit there, trying to sort through the jumble of emotions that I feel. One feeling in particular rises to the top: failure. I failed my company. I failed Renee. I failed my dad, who trusted me to lead after he was gone. Maybe he was wrong to trust me. Maybe I'm just not capable of doing this job, of making the hard decisions needed for this company to succeed.

An hour later, I'm called into the boardroom. I know what's coming.

When I walk into the boardroom, it isn't just Michael and our legal counsel; it's the entire board. I'm immediately on high alert. What the fuck is Michael up to now? Michael meets me outside the boardroom door. "Listen, I know what this looks like, but it's not what you think. Have you seen the news this morning?"

"Yes, of course, I saw it. I had no idea she was going to do that."

"I found out late yesterday that Renee Johnson was going to be interviewed on *Morning Today*, and while they couldn't tell me what about, they did indicate that it might have something to do with LyonTech. It seems Johnson violated her NDA to go on national television and call us the face of unethical Big Tech. It's a nightmare. We need all hands on deck to counter this attack."

I walk into the boardroom, stunned. I knew that Renee was anxious for us to take action, but I had no idea that this is what she had planned.

Jeffery is in mid-rant. "We had a contract! Once she signed that agreement, we owned that patent, and we decide how it's used and who to sell it to."

"I agree. Legally, we have the right of way here. She has no legal standing on this matter. I think we need to sue her." Lane Whitmore, an old friend of my father's who has been on the board for nearly twenty years, sits back in her chair in her perfectly starched grey pantsuit.

Board members nod in agreement. They barely acknowledge my arrival when I enter the room. It's clear the decision has been made without me. I've been summoned merely as a formality. I'd be pissed off if I wasn't still reeling from watching Renee's interview. It's only once our legal counsel begins talking about drawing up a suit that I realize I need to take action to stop this. If LyonTech sues Renee, she'll be destroyed. They won't stop until she's never able to work in tech again.

"Hold on. I have a better solution."

Finally, everyone turns to look at me. A few other old guards roll their eyes ready to outright dismiss me. Others look somewhat curious to hear what I have to say.

"As you all know, Renee and I co-founded a firm together five years ago. I think I can convince her to drop her campaign against us and stand down. Suing her will only make us look like a bully. We'll martyr her and only convince the public that she's right and join her cause. We need to find a quiet way to make this go away. Let me handle it."

For a moment, everyone is silent, thinking it over. Michael looks at me and nods. "He's right. A lawsuit will only play in her favor. Let's see if Knox can finesse this. But if it doesn't work, then we'll go after her hard. Knox, we'll give you two days to make this go away before we take legal action. But if she doesn't stand down, we'll make an example of her so that no other designers think they can get away with throwing tantrums when they decide they don't like how we use their designs."

I grit my teeth and nod at Michael. "I'll take care of it."

I have no idea how I'm going to convince Renee to stand down. If she went this far to make a case against LyonTech, she thought it through and knew the consequences. She's decided that she doesn't care about what she might lose. When Renee is operating with that level of conviction, there's no talking her out of it. But I hope that I can find a way.

Chapter 20

RENEE

THE FRONT DOOR SLAMS SHUT, announcing Knox's arrival home. I don't turn away from the kitchen sink where I've just finished unloading the dishwasher, but I know what's coming. I'm placing spoons, knives, and forks back into their separate sections of the utensil organizer, preparing for the inevitable. When I got the call from *Morning Today* agreeing to interview me, I said yes without hesitation. It wasn't until I was sitting in the dressing room readying to go on air, reviewing the talking points that Marla at Autistics United helped prepare, that I knew this could be the end of my friendship with Knox. I know how much it means to him to prove that he can take over for his father as CEO. But for the first time since I met Knox seven years ago, I want something more than I want to be his friend and to see him look at me with those laughing brown eyes. I want to stand up for something more important.

To stand up for justice.

Unfortunately, Knox and his company are standing in the

way. I couldn't turn down the interview. It was the only way to really get their attention. It was the only way to force him to take action. I knew that if Knox had it his way, he would just compromise and compromise until my demands were whittled down to nothing. He'd explain it away so logically, like he had tried his best but the best he could do was some minor concession that didn't come close to what I was demanding. And nothing short of completely discontinuing the Calm Monitor will be enough.

"What were you thinking?" I hear his incredulous voice.

It's like he couldn't imagine I was even capable of doing something so huge on my own. Taking such a big, bold step, solo, has never been my style. Knox was always the bold one. The one thinking about big, flashy ideas that would propel our work into the public eye. I was always behind the scenes, focused on the work. I never wanted to do media interviews or public launch events; that was always his style. I had no problem with him being the face of our company for that reason. But this morning, I went on national television and called out the biggest tech company in the world. It was terrifying and necessary and I don't have any regrets.

The AU leaders were pleased with the interview. As soon as it aired, they started getting calls from other media outlets. Their social media blew up. A petition to have the Calm Monitor discontinued hit more than one hundred thousand signatures in under an hour, and law enforcement agencies across the country are getting calls demanding to know why they plan to target and surveil the most vulnerable disabled citizens. We anticipate not all, but some, will cancel their contracts with LyonTech.

But hearing the hurt and shock in Knox's voice right now makes my stomach knot. I wanted this to work. I wanted to make things right. But I didn't want to hurt him in the process.

With no more silverware to organize, I finally turn to him. His face is thunderous. He's never looked at me like this before.

"I'm sorry, Knox, but I couldn't just sit back and wait for you to decide how to handle this."

His face goes slack and a coldness takes over his eyes for a moment. He looks away from me and shakes his head. "You had to take action," he says. "I guess it didn't matter how it would affect me. Did you even think for a second how this would make me look?"

My eyebrows shoot up. "That's what you're worried about? How this will make you look? Well, how about the fact that I had to learn from a member of your staff that you hadn't canceled the Caldwell contract? Did you think for a second about how it would affect me if you moved forward with this? What about the people who would be harmed by your manufacturing of surveillance tools? Did you think about that?" I shake my head and turn away to begin refolding dish towels, just to have something to do with my hands.

"All you care about is your own image and protecting your father's legacy," I say. "Well, you know what? I care about my legacy too, and I can't live with the fact that something I designed could cause so much harm."

"I told you I would handle it!"

"How? How were you going to handle it?"

"I don't know! I … I was working on it. I could have put something into the contract to streamline its use or postponed the manufacturing process for a year to buy more time, just until after I…"

"Until after you what? Prove that you're the CEO your daddy knew you could be? It always comes back to you. Your image. Proving that you're good enough. You've always been good enough, Knox. I couldn't wait for you to figure that out and decide to do the right thing."

Knox just shakes his head. It's like my words haven't even

registered. "You have no idea what you've done. Me and my 'daddy issues' are all that's standing between you and a lawsuit. You have to stand down."

The rage that boils inside me seems to come out of nowhere. I slap my hand on the marble countertop and feel the heat that rises through my palm.

"You have to stay out of my way. I don't need you to save me. I never did! So stop trying." I'm on fire. I've never yelled at him before. The force of my words pushes him back a step. I can't remember the last time I felt this much anger toward someone I love. I tend to be passive and accommodating. Always trying not to be a problem. Always apologizing for my "issues." Wanting to prove that loving me doesn't have to be a time and energy suck.

A sacrifice.

But I'm done with passive. I'm done being patient. I'm done waiting for Knox to swoop in and save me.

Knox throws his hands up. "I can't talk to you when you're like this. We can discuss this when you're calm."

I quickly walk away and head into the guest bedroom as the heat continues to move up my neck and cover my face. I can't believe he just spoke to me like I'm a child. Like I can't handle my emotions. I'm boiling with so much emotion, I can't even speak.

I'm breathing heavily and I pace the floor for a moment, attempting to make sense of what just happened and what I need to do next. I have to get out here.

The repairs on my apartment are not quite done, but most of the damage was to the main living / dining area. My bedroom is fine. I can just camp out there for a while until it's done. I start packing my bag, determined to get as far away from Knox as I can. Am I running away again or am I deciding to stand on my own two feet? I couldn't decide back when I moved out of our apartment, but right now I'm certain that I'm standing on my own. No net, no Knox below to catch me as I fall. If I crash, I get back up. I have to believe that I've built myself strong enough over the last four years without him.

Knox is in the kitchen when I stomp back out of the guest room with my overnight bag and head straight for the front door.

"Renee, where are you going?" he demands.

I let the door slam behind me and race out of his building. It's only when I'm on the sidewalk that I allow the tears to fall, my heart aching because this hurts worse than when I moved out and, somehow, even worse than when he left the company. It feels like this time might truly be the end of our relationship.

Chapter 21

RENEE

I TAKE a deep breath and turn the key to the front door, preparing myself for what I will find on the other side. I've only been back to my house a few times to meet with the contractors, to talk through the list of repairs and timelines. I brace myself as I open the front door and then release it as I look around my living room. Relief hits me instantly. It's not as bad as I thought. They seem to be ahead of schedule on getting the work done.

Standing in the empty room reminds me of when I first moved into this house. I remember standing in the middle of the room and thinking of all the possibilities. The life I would create for myself here. After moving out of the apartment I shared with Knox, I moved into a tiny studio apartment with walls so thin, it felt like I could hear every breath, every step my neighbors took. I hated it, but it was cheap and I found it quickly. In two years, I was able to save enough for the down payment on my townhouse. The first place I could truly call my own. My home. A place to take off the mask that I wear every day when I move through the world. A place where I have nothing to prove. Here, I found quiet and softness and refuge from the world.

The floors have been restored and I can see where the walls have been repaired. The recently laid plaster has dried. The hole in the ceiling is closed and covered. Just a paint job, and then I can move my furniture back in.

Everything broken can be fixed. But then I think of me and Knox. We tried to fix it, or maybe we just attempted to paint over the damage and ignored what was really broken underneath.

I sigh and head up the stairs to my bedroom. I've missed being in my own space. The feel of my own sheets, familiar smells, and quiet. The minute I step into my sacred space, my entire body begins to relax. Suddenly, the tightness with which I've been holding myself begins to melt away, and as I sink onto my bed, I give myself over to the swirling mix of emotions bubbling up inside me. Weighty warmth invades me and tears fall down my cheeks. I let myself fall apart, trusting that in the morning I'll wake up and begin to rebuild.

Morning comes, and just before I open my eyes, I forget that I'm no longer at Knox's place. I expect to hear him in the kitchen making coffee after his morning workout. But then I remember the night before. I can still see his face filled with disappointment and anger. I can't remember a time when Knox has ever been angry at me, and I feel shame knowing that I made him feel that way. But I quickly shake it off. Why should I feel ashamed? He was the one who failed to follow through on what he committed to doing. He was the one who let me down. I took responsibility for my part in designing the Calm Monitor. I did what needed to be done to make things right. I wish it didn't mean hurting him in the process.

I head back out into my living room and look around at the empty space, the nearly completed repairs. Reconstruction can be an opportunity to make different design choices.

What if I decided to reconstruct my life?

Chapter 22

KNOX

THE HOT TEXAS air feels like a heating pad wrapped around my head. I feel its thickness everywhere. You'd think after a lifetime of living here, I'd be used to it. But today it feels especially constricting. I drive along the flat stretch of interstate to my parents' house. As I leave the city limits, an expanse of barren, dried-up land extends before me. Sometimes it feels like a straight line from growing up in Prairie Wood to my life in Austin, but then I remember all the twists and turns and near collisions that had to happen for me to get here. But as I drive back home to visit my mom, I wonder if I ever truly left.

When I left home, I thought I was leaving behind the life my parents had planned for me. I thought I was giving up the perfectly planned, neatly defined future that felt just as constricting as this thick July heat. I didn't want to work for my dad. I left that future behind to carve out my own path. Along the way, I found Renee and we built something together. Something that I could proudly call my own. For a minute, I looked at my life and saw the company I was building alongside my best friend and thought I had escaped the expectations that they set for me. I was proud to be my own man; I was out of his shadow and standing in my own light. But then I got the call that changed everything.

We were two years into building Renox Tech. We'd just moved into our first office space—a tiny little two-person box inside a coworking space in downtown Austin. It was shaped like a rectangle. Renee and I sat with our backs to each other. The space was so narrow, we could barely push back our office chairs without bumping into each other. The glass window looked out into a hallway facing other small cubes. It was tight and windowless, but we loved it. Renee liked to keep the lights low, so we rarely turned on the overhead fluorescents, mostly working in the dim light from the hall or turning on the small desk lamp she bought from a flea market when we first moved in and needed some office furniture. It was a cocoon of a space and we were growing something inside it. She designed and I managed the business, built partnerships, developed sales plans and marketing campaigns. We each knew our lane and trusted each other completely.

It was an ordinary Wednesday when I got the call. Renee was in one of her deep work modes, hyper-focused on our latest project, and I didn't want to disturb her, so the moment I heard my phone vibrate on my desk, I snatched it up and went out into the hallway before looking at the caller ID. I was surprised to see that it was my dad. Ever since I made it clear that I wasn't going to work for him, our relationship had changed. He never said he was disappointed, but the tension between us was evident. If he was calling me, something was wrong.

"Dad? Everything okay?"

There was a pause on the other line before he cleared his throat to speak. "Hey, son, we need to talk…"

The solemn tone behind those words made my stomach drop. I held my breath as I listened to him tell me about his cancer, the word "terminal" reverberating in my ears like a gong. Everything else turned to static after that.

The news brought me to my knees. Learning that he was going to die changed everything. Suddenly what I wanted seemed meaningless. What did my life, my dreams, mean when the person who gave me everything was dying? When the one who gave me a chance at life was leaving this Earth and all he wanted was for me to take care of the thing he built? The company that he'd poured more than thirty years of his life into. I would have said yes to anything he asked of me. I would have protected any part of him I could keep. The realization startled me. It was like I had no idea until that moment just how much I loved and longed to keep my dad.

Now he's gone. And here I am, taking care of his things and retracing my steps, wondering how I got here. If it's all even worth it. My parents' house finally comes into view after a two-hour drive. Their two-story English Victorian sits in the middle of a suburban cul-de-sac. As I pull up to the driveway, it occurs to me how little I visit anymore. My mom has been living here in this oversized house all alone for nearly a year.

I use my key and walk inside. The faint smell of vanilla and lavender hits my nose immediately. It's quiet and cool. The air conditioning provides immediate relief from the overbearing heat.

"Mom?" I call out. But there's no reply. She's not here. I didn't think to call before I drove here. I just needed to get out of the city. I walk through the hall, past the formal dining room, toward the kitchen. The walls are still covered in family photos. Most of me at every stage of my life. Little League, football, and graduations from kindergarten to college. I stop at a photo of me and Dad. We're both beaming at the camera, heads leaned toward each other, arms slung over each other's shoulders. I recognize it from my sophomore year of high school. A time when all I ever wanted was to be just like him, to be everything he wanted me to be. I continue into the kitchen. I don't think this house has ever felt so big and so empty. Why does my mom stay? Why not just sell the house? I guess for the same reasons I'm here. It's the only place left where I can find him.

I head up to his office and sit behind his broad mahogany desk. The wood still shines like it's cleaned regularly, as if he just might return to sit here again. I remember peeking into his office door at night when I was supposed to be in bed to watch him work. I didn't understand what he did, but I knew that this room with its wall full of books on one side and another full of plaques and awards on the other made him seem bigger than life, like he was the most important man in the world. I wanted to be just as important someday.

As I sit behind his desk, a man with the same title he once held, I don't feel as important or as big as he once was.

Did I really think it would be that easy?

Or maybe I trusted him more than I trusted myself when I agreed to fill his shoes. I sigh and lean back in his chair. I'm taking in the neatly organized desk when I notice a file with my name on it peeking out of a slightly open drawer. I pull it out hesitantly. Holding my breath. Wondering what he could have possibly left for me here. For a moment, I dread opening it. Inside are documents that, at first glance, make no sense to me. But I do notice the names of board members along with their signed conflict-of-interest disclosures. Another set of documents that look like financial reports. I put the file aside to look more closely at it later.

I lean back in his leather high-back chair and swivel to face the window, expecting to see the same neatly manicured green grass that I used to run end to end most days. Instead, I see even parallel rows of plants spread out like a blanket in the center of the yard. I gasp at the sight and for a moment I'm transported back to Renee's mom's house in Berkeley. What is this? The change is so dramatic, it's disorienting. I race down the stairs to the backyard, needing to see it up close. Here I thought my mother was grieving and instead she was growing a garden?

It is only once I'm outside that I see her, dressed in loose-fitting jeans and one of my dad's old button-down shirts—wrinkled and rolled at the sleeves—with a straw hat on her head, humming to herself, down on her knees in the soil. I'm mesmerized by the sight. I don't think I've seen my mother dirty or in anything less than a perfect dress fit for a CEO's wife.

"Mom?"

Her head pops up and her eyes are alight with surprise. "Son! What a surprise!" She jumps up from her spot, pulling off her gardening gloves and dusting off her knees, and she makes her way to me. For some reason, her lightness and joy feel out of place. I think I've had an image of her in my mind, sitting here quietly and mourning her dead husband, shrouded in black.

She wraps me in a hug and I lean into the pressure. The woman is small and looks so fragile, but she hugs like a man twice her size. A tiny bear hug. It's only when I lean into her, dropping my chin onto her shoulder, breathing in her familiar scent of lavender mixed with the unfamiliar earthy smell of dirt and a bit of sweat, that I realize how much I've needed her. How much I've missed my mom. She pulls back from the embrace to look me up and down, her brown eyes assessing with a knowing look.

"So you finally came to see your old mom."

I'm a bit ashamed that it's taken me so long. I haven't been back here in months. I helped her handle some of my father's financial affairs a month after the funeral and I haven't been back since. That was four months ago.

"I'm sorry, Mom. It's been a lot getting settled into my role at LyonTech."

She sighs heavily and turns back toward her garden. "Uh, LyonTech." She softly shakes her head, staring off past the garden as if remembering something. "Did you know your father never wanted me to have a garden? He hated the mess of it. He liked things to be neat and tidy at all times."

I stare at the side of her head like she's been body snatched and I'm listening to an alien speak. I've never heard my mother say anything contradictory about my father. They always seemed united on everything. She wasn't exactly submissive, but she was always on his side.

"There were lots of ways he dictated what our life should look like, and since he was the primary breadwinner, I felt like I should support him and just go along with it. But you finally stood up to him and told him you were going to choose your own path…" She turns to me with a crooked grin. "I was so proud of you, and that was the one time I pushed back. I might not have pushed for the things I wanted. But for … I would fight him for you. That was one of the few times when we really fought."

I'm stunned and unable to process any of this. It's like I'm meeting my mother for the first time.

"You didn't have to do that, Mom."

"Yes, I did. I had to do it for all the times you wanted to take an art class and he wanted you to play a sport. All the times you wanted to just hang out with friends and he insisted that you make more productive use of your time. All the times he pressured you to follow in his footsteps and I stood back and watched you struggle. Struggle to make him proud and still try to be your own person.

"When he died, I sat here in this house. Getting up, day after day, following the same routines he set in place. I was still playing the part of his supportive wife and he wasn't even here anymore. And then, one morning, I was sitting in the kitchen, drinking coffee, staring out at this empty unused backyard, and I decided: enough. The dead don't get to dictate our lives. I want a garden. So I made a garden."

We both stare silently at her handiwork. "It's a beautiful garden, Mom."

"Thank you, son. Are you hungry? You look hungry. Let's make some lunch and you can tell me what's weighing on your heart." And together, we head into the kitchen to make sandwiches and lemonade.

We return to the back patio overlooking my mother's garden and chat over sandwiches, hers a dainty turkey sandwich with tomato and Swiss, mine a triple-stack stuffed full of meat and provolone, lettuce and tomato, the way my dad and I used to eat it every Sunday afternoon while watching football together. The green salad is a colorful medley of ripe tomatoes; crisp cucumbers; bright, juicy peach slices; and sunflower seeds.

We make small talk over our meal, talking about an endless supply of mundane things, never venturing into the dim corners where our shared loss might shroud this easy summer day. I watch my mother from across the table, the easy way she moves. Her dark-brown hair is pulled into a loose knot at the top of her head. Simple brown tortoiseshell sunglasses are propped up on her head, and her body is relaxed, slouching into the oversized vinyl chair couch, her bare feet propped up on the chair next to her. Her caramel skin is bright, showing off the laugh lines around her mouth I never noticed before. She reminds me a little of Renee's mom, who lives in her garden or the woods beyond it, never far from the land. It's like my father's death has unlocked something within her. Given her permission to be free in a way she never was before and seeing her in this way makes something knot up tightly in my gut. I don't want to name it. It feels too much like resentment, and I know she doesn't deserve that.

In fact, I know it's not her that I resent.

"I don't know what I'm doing, Mom. I'm beginning to think it was a mistake to take over the company."

She turns to look at me and I don't know what I was expecting to see in her eyes. Disappointment, maybe, or surprise, but instead she smiles softly at me and just nods. She reaches across the table and takes my hands and hers and says, "Baby, he's gone. It took me a while to be able to admit that to myself. That he's not here. He's not going to walk out into the backyard and say, 'What have you done to my lawn?' He's not going to demand I give back his dress shirt. He's not going to remind me about the dinner party we need to attend so he can court a new client. He is not here anymore. And how we live with that is up to us. Grief isn't something you can escape; you just learn to live with it. Missing him is a part of me. But there's nothing that we can do to bring him back."

I stare at the crumbs of my empty plate, trying to push back the tears burning my eyes, and let her words reverberate through me. Do I really know it? Or have I been doing what I've always done, which is to try to be good? Try to be everything he wanted me to be in the hopes that he'll be proud of me? Who am I when I'm not trying to prove something to my father?

As if reading my thoughts, she says, "The best way you can honor your father is to honor yourself and what matters to you."

After lunch, she walks me to the door.

"I think if your father were here, he would say that you are his greatest legacy, not that company. Remember that."

On the drive back to Austin, I feel a little lighter but not quite clear on my next move. But one thing I know for sure: if I'm going to commit to running LyonTech, I have to do it my way and stop trying to fill his shoes when it means ignoring his failures as a leader.

Chapter 23

RENEE

THIS IS the third time I've repacked this box of books, removing them and placing them back into the boxes in different configurations, but each time, when I'm almost ready to seal it and move on to the next box, I feel the buzzing. It's subtle at first. My stomach tightens, my shoulders wrench up a little higher, and my breath becomes shallow because I know that if I don't unpack this box and do it again, the buzzing feeling will grow stronger until it's like my chest is filled with a hive of bees compressing on my diaphragm so much I can't breathe—and I will not have a meltdown today. I promised myself that this morning when I left the house and made my way to my office for the very last time, to pack everything and close the company that I spent the last five years building. I promised myself that I would do it without falling apart. But I'm stuck in an interminable loop because the books in this box don't fit together neatly. It's the larger coffee-table-style book on iconography; it's sticking out alongside the smaller books. I snatch it out of the box and arrange the smaller books on one side with the larger hardbacks stacked on their spines, and now everything fits. It's neat and balanced; every book fits in place like a puzzle. Better. I breathe. The buzzing stills for a moment. I close the box and tape it shut.

I need to remind myself why I'm doing this. I have no doubt it's the right choice. I love designing but I hated running a company. Selling Renox was the best decision I could have made for myself and for my team. I can admit that I was a terrible boss. Not because I was cruel or abusive, but because I just didn't want to be a boss. Reconstructing my life means deciding the things that I no longer want to do. Renox was a dream that I shared with Knox. We were going to build this company together, but when he left, I found myself trying to hold it together. Trying to hold on to that one piece of us that I still had left. Deciding to let it go was like a ten-ton weight lifted off my back.

"Found it!" Jordyn yells triumphantly, pulling me from my thoughts. She holds up the hairbrush she lost in the office six months ago. I shake my head as I move on to the next box of books, praying this one doesn't take twenty minutes to get right. At this rate, I'll be here for a month trying to get everything packed just right, but I don't have a month. The movers will be here in two hours. "It was in the bottom of my desk drawer all this time."

I finish sealing the box in front of me before turning to Jordyn. "And to think you blamed poor Mitchell for stealing it."

"He was the most likely suspect."

"How? He was bald. Why would he steal your hairbrush?"

"For his shaggy hipster beard. You know how those guys are about their beards. Always grooming it. I bet he had a six-part beard-grooming routine at night."

"You should track Mitchell down and apologize to him."

Jordyn looks over her tortoiseshell glasses at me with raised eyebrows and, pausing for effect, says, "Not a chance. I never trusted that kid. Even if he didn't steal my hairbrush, I know he was up to something sneaky. Just never caught him." Jordyn flips her hair, which is dyed a bright red color this week, and floats away in her Jordyn way.

Mitchell was an excellent UX designer whom I recruited fresh out of college. Now that Renox has been subsumed by Advance Tech, he's starting a new job but working on many of the same projects he did for Renox, just in a much nicer officer with a huge pay increase. When I sold to Advance, I made sure that my team wasn't just protected but that they would receive the kinds of salaries, bonuses, and stock options I could never offer them. They were all disappointed to hear that Renox was closing, but when I told them about their new packages and how they'd be building their very own edutech department for Advance, they got really excited. Knowing that they would end up in much better positions once we closed our doors alleviated the guilt I felt at giving up. But it's the right thing to do.

I finally lift my head from the box of books I'm packing to look over at Jordyn and roll my eyes. But she's too busy picking lint out of her newly recovered hairbrush to notice. Looking around the office, I can see that we're just about through packing. The empty desks are spread out across the open-floor-plan office, and the kitchen counter is no longer cluttered with coffeepots, mugs, and dish racks. My glass cube of an office set apart from the rest of the room, always on the edge of all the action, just watching, never stepping into the whirl of chatter, brainstorming, and collaboration. It's a relief to no longer feel the pressure to participate. Wondering if I'm saying the wrong thing or pushing my own ideas so passionately that it shuts down the creative process. It's not that I don't want to collaborate with others. I do. I long for it. But being so self-conscious about my role created a tension that always left me feeling exhausted by the effort.

My office now sits completely empty, the glass scrubbed clean of all the ideas I needed to get out of my brain and onto the wall. The only thing left is my desk lamp. It's an old lamp that looks completely out of place in our modern office. It looks more like it should be in the drawing room of some old Victorian house. It's a throwback from the very first workspace Knox and I shared. A tiny coworking space in East Austin. And it's the one item I've somehow ignored and avoided touching in all the packing. I can't decide what to do with it. Do I pack it and store it, toss it out, or take it home?

In the next two hours, the movers will be here to pick up the rest of the boxes, and then that's it. The offices of Renox Tech will be closing their doors. It still hasn't quite hit me. Like most things, it will take a while for the realization to settle upon me. The realization that, after five years of blood, sweat, and tears, my company is closing its doors for good.

This was a dream that started seven years ago while I was still an undergrad at UT Austin. I wanted to develop tech solutions for the education sector. I wanted to improve the educational experiences of all kids, but especially neurodivergent kids like me who needed a little bit more help to thrive in school. But it takes a lot more than a dream to make a business successful.

"You're doing it again," Jordyn calls.

"Doing what?"

"That thing where you zone out and stare into space, thinking really deep thoughts or astral traveling to another plane of reality or whatever you do in that brilliant mind of yours."

Using the teacher voice she's perfected, she adds, "Please share your thoughts with the class, Ms. Johnson."

"I was just taking inventory. Trying to figure out what's left to pack before the movers get here." That's the safe answer. The harder answer is that I have no idea how I feel yet. There's a deep, gaping hole in my chest where this company used to live, and I have no idea what I will replace it with. For five years, all I've done is work. Who am I when I'm not putting every ounce of my effort into running this company? I guess I'm about to find out.

The part that is much more difficult to accept is that this is the last piece of Knox I have left. Just thinking of him expands the growing pressure against my chest. We haven't spoken in over a month. Not since I ran out of his apartment ready to explode. I breathe through it, knowing that it will only make Jordyn even more vigilant about trying to take care of me. I just want to finish packing up the office and head home, where I can fall apart quietly and alone without anyone to witness.

"You know, I'm really proud of you for doing this," she says softly. "You're moving on. You're way too young to be stuck doing work you don't want to do, and I could tell you hated running this company."

"I didn't hate it," I counter. "I loved the work we did. The whole Calm Monitor situation definitely made me rethink a lot of things. But for the most part, I think we did great work."

"But Knox was supposed to handle the business side."

"Yeah. His leaving certainly changed things," I say, busying myself with building another box.

Cautiously, she asks, "Have you spoken to him since the interview?" I pretend to ignore her as I aggressively remove the last of the books on the shelf and shove them into boxes. "I just think maybe this is a good time to talk. Maybe hear his side of things…"

"I don't want to talk about Knox," I respond way too sharply. I can feel that pressure on my chest getting heavier, my breathing speeding up. Jaw tight. Hands clenching. I quickly turn away from Jordyn, crossing to the other side of the now-empty room to face the window, and calm myself.

"It's okay," Jordyn says in a soothing tone. But it's not okay.

Nothing is okay right now. My whole world has collapsed around me and I have no choice but to watch the pieces fall at my feet.

Jordyn drops the conversation but continues to peek over at me to make sure I'm okay. I hide from her behind my desk, double checking that nothing is left in the drawers. I find something thin, smooth, and wide stuck inside the bottom drawer of my desk and pull at it until it comes free. It's a photo of me, Jordyn, and Knox from our graduation day. I'm between the two of them, their arms wrapped around me on both sides, my face slightly turned away from the camera and smiling off into the distance. Knox is looking at me with laughter in his eyes. Jordyn is the only one who seems to be conscious of the camera, giving her best angles while looking directly into the lens.

I put the picture in my back pocket, begin taping all the desk drawers shut, and continue to make sure that everything is ready for the move.

The movers arrive and quickly load up all the office furniture and boxes that haven't already been donated. Jordyn stands close by, surely itching to comfort me but knowing full well that I'd swat her hands away if she starts trying to hug me. There's no need to soothe me, as much as I know she wants to. I don't need soothing. I've made my choice. This was the right choice. It might be the first time in my life that I put myself first. Made a decision that would change the course of my life without waiting for someone else to give me approval. To tell me what to do. I stand in the middle of my now-empty office space, allowing myself to truly take in the finality of this moment. I need to remember this feeling. This feeling of truly trusting myself.

I clutch my office lamp to my side as we watch the movers drive away. Jordyn turns to me. "I'm so glad that you're taking some time off."

I glance her way, knowing that there's more of a question in that statement. She wants to know if I've changed my mind about taking a sabbatical. Jordyn and my parents have all been pushing for this. They think I need to rest. They know transition can be hard for me and they've concluded that a six-month break is exactly what I need to decide what I want to do next and slowly transition at a pace that's right for me. Hearing the concern in her voice, I expect to feel defensive. I expect to want to push away her concern. But instead, I just feel grateful to know that I have people who want the best for me.

"I haven't changed my mind. I am still going to take the time off. But I appreciate you looking out for me."

Jordyn nods, shrugs, and smiles. "Always."

I turn to her. "Really, Jordyn, thank you."

Her eyebrows shoot up in surprise. She smiles curiously. "For what?"

"For being such a good friend. For always having my back." I pull her into a hug. She goes slack with surprise. I'm not a touchy-feely kind of friend. I don't ever initiate hugs. But then she embraces me back and leans into it.

"I'm proud of you," she tells me.

I laugh and say, "Yeah, I'm proud of me too."

Chapter 24

KNOX

"ARE YOU READY?"

Ready? Am I ready? Was I ready six months ago when I was named CEO shortly after my father's death? Am I ready now that I've taken an honest look at LyonTech and discovered that the man I revered, the father I was so in awe of most of my life, was not the blueprint for leadership I believed he was?

Becoming the leader this company needs—the leader I want to be—requires that I make some hard choices. Choices that will almost certainly put me in opposition to his legacy. I spent all night tossing and turning, agonizing over what today would bring. Wondering if I was betraying him. But if my mother can tear up the lawn of the house he built for her and create a garden, then I can do what needs to be done to set a new course for this company, even if it means undoing some of my father's work. Maybe that's not what he had in mind when he implored me to take over for him, but he had to know I would make changes, right?

My mind is circling with unanswered questions, but I know I can't betray myself and the people I care about all so that I can fulfill a dead man's final plea. I turn to Sam Harris, my new COO, and nod. In the two weeks since I promoted her, she's already brought so many fresh ideas and new approaches to supporting our staff of five hundred people nationwide. It's ridiculous she wasn't promoted sooner. Promoting her from the New York office was the first decision I made that was colored by guilt, obligation, and a low-grade imposter syndrome. Seeing how well she owns the role gives me the confidence I need to do what has to be done this morning.

"Yes, I'm ready. Be sure to have security on standby."

Sam nods and heads out to greet the board members as they arrive. I look around my office, which still feels like my father's office. The four walls are still covered with his choices in artwork, his awards, his photos; even the furniture is reminiscent of him. I sat in this room for the last six months attempting to be him, attempting to do my best impression of him, and I lost myself in the process. I stopped paying attention to what mattered to me.

I open my phone and pull up the text chain with Renee. My fingers itch to message her; it would be even better to hear her voice right now. Telling me what I need to hear. Fortifying me with her words, her presence. I miss her. I don't think I'll ever stop longing for her. Maybe this first step is how we can find our way back to each other … again.

I walk into the boardroom and look around the table filled with white men handpicked by my father to serve on his board. They have no idea what is about to happen, as evidenced by the smug, confident way they lean back in their chairs. Very few raise their eyes from their phones or their conversations when I enter. Before today, their disregard would have made me sweat with a churning eagerness to prove myself. Today, it doesn't burn the same way. Today, I stop trying to prove myself.

Today, I have the leverage I need to completely shift the power dynamic. I get right to it.

"Okay, I won't keep you long, but this was not something that could wait until the quarterly shareholder meeting. There's a conflict of interest that needs to be addressed." Those words seem to get their attention. All eyes turn to me.

Michael leans forward in his chair. "Uh, Knox, maybe you and I should discuss this separately first so I can address any concerns you have…"

"No, that won't be necessary, Michael."

Michael looks baffled by my easy dismissal. His mouth hangs slightly agape. Worried looks make their way around the room as I continue. "It has come to my attention that four members of this board are personally invested in the building of private residential centers for disabled children. Those sites are owned by Caldwell Homes. As you all know, LyonTech entered a multimillion-dollar contract with Caldwell to provide our Calm Monitors to all their sites nationwide. Before my father died, he suspected several of you of double-dealing, which, as you know, is not only illegal but is a breach of the conflict-of-interest agreements that you each signed when joining the board."

"Now, wait a minute, son. You can't just accuse people of breaking the law without proof," Tom Ellison says, gesturing around the table.

"I'm not accusing just anyone, Tom. I'm accusing you, along with your business partners Michael, Garrison, and Philip." The tide has turned in the room. But their outrage turns to shock when they see our building security appear outside the glass. Sam makes her way around the room, handing each man a separation agreement, effectively ending their terms as members of the board. "Now, if you'll please sign these agreements, we can avoid having to pursue legal action against you. You should also know that I've terminated the contract with Caldwell. Under the circumstances, they agreed it was important to avoid the public perception of unethical business dealings."

The four disgraced board members gather their things and leave, looking completely stunned by this turn of events. The rest of the board sits quietly, watching this unfold. Once they're out of the room, everyone turns again to me.

"If anyone else has a conflict of interest they would like to report," I say, "you should do so now because, as you can see, it will not be tolerated."

I pause and look around the room. They exchange nervous glances. A new era has arrived, and I think at this moment they all finally see it. As they leave the room, I receive more than a few appreciative nods in my direction. A newfound respect seems to have taken hold.

Jeffrey stops beside me before exiting. He extends his hand and looks me in the eye. "Well done."

And then they're gone and I feel like I take a full, deep breath for the first time since I discovered that I was being played by my own board. The documents I gathered at my father's home office were more than informative. He had suspected and even began investigating board members, but he was always a man living in his final days, exhausted but refusing to stop working until he had nothing left. This was the thing I could finish for him. Maybe it was even the reason why he wanted me to be CEO. He wanted me to uncover the truth and make it count.

In an hour, our media department will announce to the world that we ended our contract with Caldwell and all I can think about is what Renee will think. Will it be enough to convince her that I'm on her side? Will it be enough to convince her that I heard everything she said, that I really listened?

I guess I'll have to wait and see.

Chapter 25

RENEE

I'VE NEVER HAD autistic friends. It's only now, as I sit here in the AU offices during one of their monthly game-night hangs, that I realize that. I think it's because I always thought being autistic was something I needed to overcome. But spending time with the members of Autistic United over the last few months has taught me a lot about internalized ableism and the ways we autistics internalize the negative stereotypes about us.

Tonight I realize just how much I've been missing because hanging out at AU feels like the first time I can truly be myself in a social setting without needing to constantly police my own behavior and worry I might say or do the wrong thing.

The small storefront office is warmly lit, with eight AU members spread around the space. Two people have their heads down, working on a puzzle together, occasionally speaking to each other but never taking their eyes off the puzzle pieces they move around the table and slot into place. Someone else sits alone on an oversized chair with a weighted blanket over their lap, wearing noise-canceling headphones and knitting. A small group chats at the table with art supplies spread out, each working on their own drawing. No one feels compelled to do anything they don't want to do, yet the group feels so connected.

So this is what a neurodivergent hangout looks like. I sigh contentedly and sip my tea, watching and observing everyone around the room. I'm sitting on the couch with my tablet, jotting down ideas as they come to me. Being here has made me feel inspired again for the first time in a long while. What if being social could be like this all the time? What if being together didn't need to be so fraught with the tense need to find one activity that everyone does at the same time?

Marla comes over and sits on the other end of the couch. She's dyed her purple hair jet black. A white T-shirt shows off the perfectly shaded tattoos that run up her arms. "You're a badass, you know that, Renee?"

"I do not," I reply automatically.

"Well, you are, and the work that you're doing now is going to make a huge difference for our community."

I try to take in what she's saying, but I can't help the feeling of doubt. "I know. I guess I'm worried about making the same mistakes again." I want to do good. I want to create things that help and not cause more harm. But how can I be sure I'm doing that?

"We need more designers out there like you, creating aids that improve the lives of autistics and other neurodivergent people. And with the advisory group, you've ensured that you have the right people holding you accountable so you don't get stuck. Don't overthink it. You've made mistakes in the past, but you've more than repaired the damage."

I nod. She's right. Before, I made decisions based on my own experience. My own ideas. I did research and got feedback, but because of my own biases, I was looking in the wrong direction, listening for the wrong things.

I smile, breaking the momentary eye contact and feeling my chest heat from the unexpected praise. When I first walked into the AU offices for that first meeting, the criticism they had of my work cut deep. But I was willing to take it because I felt like it was the right thing to do. They called me out and I waited way too long to take responsibility for my work on the Calm Monitor. But I never expected them to embrace me the way that they have. They've invited me to join their board, and I'm even launching a new initiative under the AU banner, a disability design advisory group that will advocate for more ethical decisions in tech design for disabled communities. When I closed Renox Tech, I wasn't sure what I was going to do next, but they've welcomed me into this community and given me a new sense of purpose that aligns with who I am and what I care about. For that, I'll always be grateful.

Marla looks down at her phone to read a text and says loudly enough for the group to hear, "Turn on the TV. Lyon-Tech is doing a press conference."

My head shoots up. I hold my breath as Knox's face fills the screen. He stands behind a podium, speaking. "...so today I'm here to announce that we are discontinuing the manufacturing and distribution of the Calm Monitor and terminating our contract with Caldwell."

Everyone in the room is stunned. We stare silently at the screen, listening as Knox announces that they are meeting every one of AU's demands. But he doesn't stop there. He mentions me several times, praising my commitment to accountability. But it's the last part that leaves me breathless. In response to a question about our relationship, he looks directly into the camera and says, "Renee and I have known each other for nearly a decade. We met in college and co-founded a company, and she is and will always be one of the most important people in my life. She's also the most brilliant designer I've ever worked with and the beating heart of ethical tech. When she went on national television to take accountability for her own mistakes as a designer, she taught us all an important lesson about what true leadership looks like. I couldn't be prouder to call her my friend."

I don't even realize that I'm crying until someone gently presses a tissue into my hand.

I wipe away my tears and slump back into the couch cushions. Around the room, people are all smiles, celebrating this huge victory for AU. But for some reason, I don't feel like celebrating, and I realize that it's because, in the process, I lost my best friend.

Once the night winds down, we all begin to leave the offices to head home. Marla walks me to the door. "Congratulations," I say.

"Yeah, congratulations to you too," she replies. I nod, even though I don't feel particularly celebratory. "You know, you don't have to pick and choose. It's not either you choose us or him. You can have both."

I look up at her, surprised. It's like she's read my mind, pointing out a thing I hadn't quite articulated yet. The "either-or" of this situation. Letting go of the past so I can move forward. Even if it means letting go of Knox.

I leave the AU office and head home. I go straight to bed, wanting to sleep away the sense of loss I think I've been running from since I raced out of Knox's apartment after our argument. Seeing his face on the TV screen, the way he spoke about us … the weight of my grief over losing my best friend consumes me. But sleep doesn't offer me relief. I find myself tossing and turning throughout the night. Once the restless night finally gives way to morning, I decide I need to see him.

Chapter 26

RENEE

AS I RIDE the elevator up to his apartment, I try to figure out what I'm going to say, but my mind remains blank. By the time I'm standing in his foyer, I decide that I'll just thank him for listening, for doing the right thing, and then ... I don't know. It's too hard to admit what I really want. The admission sits heavy on my chest; to say it would be like a balloon expanding to its limit, ready to pop, releasing more than I've ever known how to express.

My inner chaos is replaced by confusion when I see all the activity happening in his place. Movers take furniture out the door and the balloon deflates, my chest caves in, and everything constricts. Is he leaving? Again?

I sidestep a mover exiting his door with a tall grey lamp that looks like some kind of post-modern minimalist sculpture and then tentatively knock at the open door. "Hello?"

Knox appears in the long hallway, trailed by a woman with

a cute, messy topknot, wearing the kind of fashionable jogging suit that you could wear to the office. I seem to be losing more and more air by the second.

When Knox sees me, his eyes light up and then he turns to her. "Would you give us a second?"

She nods and heads back into the apartment as he makes his way to the door. My stomach is in knots, and heat blooms behind my eyelids. Seeing him right now feels more difficult than I could have imagined. Maybe I shouldn't have come.

"Hey," he says.

"Thank you!" I blurt out before my lungs collapse and my chest caves in on itself. I feel like an armadillo ready to hide beneath my hard shell and protect myself from the final rejection, the final loss, the end of Renee and Knox.

He steps closer to me. "I should be thanking you. You pushed me to take action. I don't know that I would have gotten there without you."

I'm listening to his words, but I can't help but be distracted by the activity in the room behind me, the movers packing up furniture, the woman in the cool jogging suit directing them.

"Uh … are you moving?"

"Oh! No, just redecorating. Come in." He invites me in and introduces me to his interior designer: jogging suit woman.

The knot slowly begins to unravel, the balloon inflating a bit. I take a breath.

We escape the moving activities by retreating into his bedroom. He tells me about how he looked around at the monotone, sterile post-modern furniture in his penthouse and decided it was time for a change. More colors, more comfortable furniture. A homier feel. I listen quietly, taking in the relaxed look of him. It seems like so much has changed for him since we saw each other a month ago. The snug grey T-shirt he's wearing stretches across his broad chest, perfectly fitted jeans hang low on his hips, and he's even started to let his hair grow out a little more. He almost looks like the Knox I knew in college.

"Listen," I say. "I have something to say. Something I should have said a long time ago. Maybe if I had, we could have saved ourselves a lot of turmoil."

"Okay," he says, sitting down on the bed.

I lean against the wall to hold myself up. I pause for a moment and he waits patiently for me, the way he always has. I never feel the anxious need to rush to get to the point with him. I never worry that if I'm not quick enough, he'll lose interest or barrel right over me to make decisions or push the conversations forward. With Knox, silence has never felt uncomfortable.

After a moment, I still can't get my thoughts to slow down enough to say what I need to say. I growl with frustration and look up at the ceiling. "I'm sorry. I'm trying to figure out how to start." If this were a design problem, I'd know exactly where to begin. I've always been more confident in my work than in my personal life.

"It's okay, take your time. What if we just sat quietly for a minute, or we could…"

That's it, I think. "The what-if game," I blurt out. It's the way we used to brainstorm ideas together.

"You want to play the what-if game?" he asks, slightly confused.

"Just bear with me for a second, please," I plead, and he nods and waits patiently like he always has. "What if it's much easier to break things down into parts than it is to see the whole of who we are together?" I start and the balloon in my chest deflates enough that I can draw in a breath. He nods, listening and looking at me with something in his eyes I can't quite read. "What if it's easier to see everything as a problem for me to

What If...I Love You

solve, and when I was confused about my feelings for you and your feelings for me, I decided that the solution was to just leave and … for that … I'm really sorry. What if…" And this is the part that I've always struggled with. "Oh, Knox, what if … I've always loved you but didn't believe I truly knew how to love you the way you deserved?"

Before the words are out of my mouth, he's on his feet, reaching for me, embracing me, and while his warmth is steadying, I'm not done, so I continue with my head pressed to his chest. "What if, in a world of endless probabilities, I know with full certainty"—I look up into his eyes, my own brimming with tears as I say the most terrifying thing I've ever given voice to—"that I will love you for the rest of my life?"

He squeezes me tighter and the pressure feels so good, I melt into him.

I feel things for him now that I don't think I ever allowed myself to feel before.

"I love you," I admit to myself, to him, the balloon in my chest stretching, expanding, forcing my lungs to expand with the revelation.

He pulls back just enough to look at me, and in his eyes, all I see is love.

Finally, he speaks. "You are my best friend and the only woman I've ever loved. You are my home. When I'm not with you, I just feel lost. Please, baby, let me come home."

I nod as the balloon expands to the brink of bursting. I can't speak, too overcome with all the things I feel for this man, so instead, I do the thing I've always done. I wrap my arms around him and allow him to hold me tight. It's only there, surrounded by him, my face pressed to his chest, that the wildness inside me begins to settle, my breath comes easy, and I let it fly free.

"I love you, Knox. You are the only place I've ever felt safe and free." Locked together in an embrace, we both soften, meld, sync our breathing, and find comfort in a shared peace.

There are no "what-ifs" when it comes to love like this.

Only certainty.

Only us.

THE END.

Acknowledgments

In the words of Snoop Dog, I want to thank me for believing in me. Because the imposter syndrome almost convinced me to put this book on the shelf and never finish or publish it.

But here we are, and I have so many people to thank for supporting me on this journey.

Let's start with my editors.

Kate Angelella, you're a damn good editor and your feedback in the early drafts of this book made me a better writer. Thank You!

Jennifer Safrey, you came in at the end and polished this manuscript up to a nice shine to prepare for her arrival in the world. I'm sure you asked, what does she have against commas? I know, I know. I can't explain it.

To my assistant, Melissa who helped make the process of marketing and promoting a book less overwhelming. Thanks for helping me finally get that newsletter going and patiently nudging me to be more consistent with social media.

To my dear friends and chosen family, Jen, Adeeba, Tim, and Wema, who have witnessed and encouraged me on this journey to becoming an author thank you for your love and support.

A special shout out to the Autastics community. As a late diagnosed autistic, being in community with other autistics is essential on the journey to developing a positive neurodivergent self-identity. Autastics continues to be a safe space for me to explore and understand myself better. Thank You!

About the Author

Yvonne Marie is an author of contemporary romance and urban fantasy living in upstate New York. For years she dreamed up love stories in her head but was too tired and overwhelmed by the pace of life to write them down.

After being diagnosed with Autism and ADHD she discovered a roadmap to understand herself and quickly gave up trying to function in ways that depleted her creativity and embraced her lifelong dream of writing romance novels.

Now she works from her quiet home outside the city where there are stacks of books in every corner and writes diverse neurodivergent characters who overcome the debilitating obstacles the world throws at them to experience pleasure, adventure, and their own unique happily-ever-after.

Join my mailing list and receive a free short story, *Coming Home to You*

www.yvonnemariewrites.com

Autistic Led Organizations to Support

Autastic: a community centering BIPOC late diagnosed autistics
   www.autastic.com

Autistic Self-Advocacy Network
   https://autisticadvocacy.org/

Autistic Women and Nonbinary Network
   https://awnnetwork.org/

Autism in Black
   https://www.autisminblack.org/

CPSIA information can be obtained
at www.ICGtesting.com
Printed in the USA
LVHW040339140623
749584LV00005B/626

9 798987 402511